Samuel French Acting Edition

I0687898

A Masterpiece of Comic...Timing!

by Robert Caisley

SAMUELFRENCH.COM   SAMUELFRENCH.CO.UK

FOR PRODUCTION ENQUIRIES

UNITED STATES AND CANADA
Info@SamuelFrench.com
1-866-598-8449

UNITED KINGDOM AND EUROPE
Plays@SamuelFrench.co.uk
020-7255-4302

Each title is subject to availability from Samuel French, depending upon country of performance. Please be aware that *A MASTERPIECE OF COMIC...TIMING!* may not be licensed by Samuel French in your territory. Professional and amateur producers should contact the nearest Samuel French office or licensing partner to verify availability.

MUSIC USE NOTE

Licensees are solely responsible for obtaining formal written permission from copyright owners to use copyrighted music in the performance of this play and are strongly cautioned to do so. If no such permission is obtained by the licensee, then the licensee must use only original music that the licensee owns and controls. Licensees are solely responsible and liable for all music clearances and shall indemnify the copyright owners of the play(s) and their licensing agent, Samuel French, against any costs, expenses, losses and liabilities arising from the use of music by licensees. Please contact the appropriate music licensing authority in your territory for the rights to any incidental music.

IMPORTANT BILLING AND CREDIT REQUIREMENTS

If you have obtained performance rights to this title, please refer to your licensing agreement for important billing and credit requirements.

"A MASTERPIECE OF COMIC...TIMING!" received its World Premiere at B Street Theatre (Buck Busfield, Producing Artistic Director) in Sacramento, California, on March 6, 2016. The director was Buck Busfield, with scenic design by Samantha Reno, lighting design by Jerry Montoya, and costumes by Gina Coyle. The Stage Manager was Lynnae Vana. The cast was as follows:

JERRY COBB......................................Dave Pierini

CHARLIE BASCHER...........................Andy Lee-Hillstrom

DANNY "NEBRASKA" JONES.....................Jason Kuykendall

NOLA HART..................................Elisabeth Nunziato

CHARACTERS

JERRY COBB – a producer, late-forties to late-fifties, prone to perspiration, foul moods, and cardiac arrest

CHARLIE BASCHER – his eager-beaver assistant, mid-twenties to late-twenties

DANNY "NEBRASKA" JONES – a neurotic writer, mid-thirties

NOLA HART – Danny's ex, a middle-aged femme fatale, aspiring to always be cast as the ingénue

SETTING

The play is set at the Royal Palms Hotel
Scottsdale, Arizona
1963

ACT ONE

Scene One: A Monday in July
Scene Two: The following morning, around ten o'clock
Scene Three: The next morning, just past noon

ACT TWO

In the wee hours of the morning, the next day

ACKNOWLEDGEMENTS

The author wishes to thank Buck Busfield, Jere Hodgin, Roy Steinberg, Craig Miller, the Idaho Commission on the Arts, and the National Endowment for the Arts for their support during the writing of this play.

"I understand your new play is full of single entendres."

– George S. Kaufman

For Mom

ACT ONE

Scene One

(A very well-appointed suite at a beautiful desert resort – The Royal Palms in Scottsdale, Arizona – one of those capacious old luxury hotel rooms divided into separate living areas – one for sleeping, and one for lounging around and entertaining. But what we're privy to onstage is the living area – the bedroom and en suite bathroom are off through a doorway/hallway, right.)

(It's a blisteringly hot Monday in mid-July, and as the play begins, the air conditioning in this particular suite has gone kaput; and the ceiling fans are not turning.)

(AT RISE: **JERRY COBB** *is standing in the middle of the suite tossing a sofa cushion repeatedly up at the large overhead fan in the room. He is dripping with sweat, and despite the heat, he is dressed to the nines in a gorgeous cream linen suit – albeit soaking right through it. He tosses the seat cushion once, twice, three times into the air as the main door, up center, is thrown open and directly into the room comes* **CHARLIE BASCHER** *– he carries a case for a small portable typewriter.)*

COBB. You got him?

CHARLIE. Got his typewriter.

COBB. What good is a typewriter without the guy who types on it? Did you get pages? He promised me pages!

CHARLIE. Morning, Mr. Cobb. Can I ask: is this gonna be a good day or bad day?

COBB. Does it matter?

CHARLIE. I like to plan ahead.

COBB. Then it's a bad day.

CHARLIE. Every day seems to be a bad day with you, Mr. Cobb.

COBB. I like to plan ahead *too*!
(*Giving up on the sofa cushion.*) Charlie, get me something so I can whack this thing.

CHARLIE. What you wanna whack it for?

COBB. It refuses to oscillate.

CHARLIE. Don't take it personally, sir...it's an inanimate object.

COBB. I take *everything* personally...especially on days like today when the mercury level rivals my blood pressure.

CHARLIE. It's a hundred-and-twenty. That's a pretty good B.P. on the top end!

COBB. That's the bottom end.

CHARLIE. You have high blood pressure? I never knew that, sir.

COBB. Take a good look at me, Charlie!

(*He does. Beat.*)

CHARLIE. (*Crossing to window.*) I'll open a window.

COBB. Oh, sure...then the hot air *out there*'s gonna trade places with the hot air in *here*.

CHARLIE. It'll get a breeze through the place.

COBB. Charlie, they don't got breezes in Arizona. They got blow torches!

CHARLIE. (*Wiping his brow with a handkerchief.*) They say we can expect record temperatures all week.

COBB. Record temperatures?

CHARLIE. That's what they say.

COBB. Just my luck. I'm stuck in the desert with a bunch of overachievers. (*He starts waving the air with his hand.*) Can't we get some people in here to, you know, stir up the air?

CHARLIE. With palm fronds?

COBB. Yeah.

CHARLIE. And grass skirts?

COBB. Why not?

CHARLIE. Feeding you grapes?

COBB. Sounds lovely.

CHARLIE. It also sounds like the wrong century, Mr. Cobb.

COBB. *(Wistful.)* Whatever century that was… I *really* miss it.

CHARLIE. I'll have 'em send a guy up from maintenance – check the A/C.

COBB. Send up a dozen! What I'm paying for these rooms –? I want the *entire* heating and cooling staff lined up like footmen.

CHARLIE. Yes, sir, I'll make a call.

(He starts to place the call, but…)

COBB. And um… Charlie?

CHARLIE. Sir?

COBB. Be emphatic.

CHARLIE. I will, sir.

COBB. *Very* emphatic. Nothing in this life…

CHARLIE. I know.

COBB. …Nothing in this life gets done, without getting emphatic.

CHARLIE. *(Replacing the phone receiver.)* Here we go!

COBB. And not *your* kind of emphatic… *my* kinda emphatic. Your kind has a "sir" at the end, a "please" at the beginning, and too many "I'm sorry's" in the middle.

CHARLIE. I got my manners from my mother.

COBB. So it's a birth defect?

CHARLIE. No… I just like to be polite. I can't help it.

COBB. There's a name for that in the theatre.

CHARLIE. What?

COBB. A "tragic flaw."

CHARLIE. All right, Mr. Cobb. I'll work on being more assertive.

>   (**CHARLIE** *glances at the stubborn fan blades, then crosses to retrieve a golf club with a fluffy knit head cover from a bag.*)

COBB. Do me a favor, kid, skip over assertive and go right for *aggressive.*

CHARLIE. *(With club in hand.)* I'll try, sir.

COBB. Try harder. *(He yanks off the head cover.)* We're trying to impress this guy. Right?

CHARLIE. *(Poking at the fan blades with the club.)* That's right.

COBB. We're trying to get him on our team, yeah? The Jerry and Charlie Team.

CHARLIE. Yeah.

COBB. The *producing* team of Cobb & Bascher.

CHARLIE. *("I am not worthy.")* Mr. Cobb...

COBB. You like the sound of that? You play your cards right, kid...and this is your ticket.

CHARLIE. Yes, sir, Mr. Cobb.

COBB. This is showtime. This is *go* time! It's all about impressions. It's all about *sparkle.*

CHARLIE. Sparkle?

COBB. ...It's all about catering to the whims, proclivities, and appetites of the most despicable people on the face of the planet.

| **CHARLIE**. | **COBB**. |
| The IRS? | Writers! |

CHARLIE. Writers?

COBB. You thought I was gonna say the IRS, didn't ya? That's a thing I do. Some would call it disinformation. I call it *sparkle.*

CHARLIE. But you're a man of The Great White Way. An East Coaster, *old* Broadway – historically we like our writers.

COBB. Charlie, I wanna do what everyone else in theatre

wants to do but pretends they don't. I wanna make enough money and a name for myself on the right coast, so I can pick up and move to the left coast. I love Broadway only inasmuch as it will make Hollywood love me more. Hollywood – where they historically hate their writers. But they cover it up with *sparkle* and... overpriced salads.

CHARLIE. Do they really hate writers that much in Hollywood?

COBB. They hate 'em so much out there Charlie, they keep 'em all on lists: the A-List, the B-List, the Black List, the Red List.

CHARLIE. What's the Red List?

COBB. Same as the Black List – except they type it in bright red ink, so you *never forget* who's on the Black List. *(Pause.)* That's *sparkle* – and we gotta do some of that this week – we can never let 'em know how much we hate 'em.

CHARLIE.	**COBB**.
(Unsure.) The writers?	The IRS.

COBB. See, I did it again.

CHARLIE. Thank you for that, Mr. Cobb. It's a valuable lesson. I never knew we were supposed to hate 'em.

COBB. I'm afraid so. I mean, we *need* them, God knows we need 'em...but we don't have to like them. It's all about the "presentation." Disinformation. There are *mirrors*...in which there is *smoke*. (**CHARLIE** *is unsure if he understands that particular reference, but he nods nonetheless.*) Details, details, details.

*(**CHARLIE** nods.)*

CHARLIE. Sparkle.

COBB. I'm glad we had this talk.
    You got the list?

CHARLIE. I got the list.

COBB. Let me see the list.

(**CHARLIE** *takes out a little notepad, tears a piece of paper from it, and hands it to* **COBB**.)

(**COBB** *reads.*) Favorite drink:

CHARLIE. *(Re: drinks table stocked with bottles.)* Bourbon. Check.

COBB. Favorite sandwich:

CHARLIE. *(Removing silver lid from a tray.)* Roast beef on Russian rye, hold the mayo, *douse* the mustard.

COBB. Good. Favorite TV show:

CHARLIE. *(Switching on the TV, we briefly hear a dog barking.)* Already tuned to the station.

(*They listen.*)

COBB. *Lassie?*

CHARLIE. Check.

COBB. Favorite book:

CHARLIE. *The Agony and the Ecstasy.* First edition. Right on his bedside table.

COBB. Nice touch.

CHARLIE. Thank you, sir.

COBB. And the...piece of resist, res – how the French say it?

CHARLIE. "Pièce de résistance."

COBB. This beautiful luxury hotel. You did good kid. *(He has to wipe his brow.)* Too bad it's an inferno in here. I told him I was bringing him to paradise, not the Ninth Circle of Hell.

CHARLIE. I'm sorry about that.

COBB. You wanna practice your emphatic?

(**CHARLIE** *crosses to a table with a hotel phone. He dials.*)

CHARLIE. Here goes. *(Into phone.)* Yeah, yeah, shuttup! I talk, you listen. This is Charlie Bascher, room 306, calling for Mr. Cobb. I'm not yelling, I'm being emphatic! First: the A/C is out.

COBB. The fans don't work.

CHARLIE. *(Into phone.)* The fans don't work.

COBB. I'm having a bad day.

CHARLIE. *(Into phone.)* Mr. Cobb is having one of his customary bad days.

> *(At the bar,* **COBB** *is disheartened to find a single, lonely, half-melted cube left in the ice bucket, which he drops, using the tongs, into his glass with a clink.)*

COBB. And we're outta ice.

CHARLIE. *(Into phone.)* Send up some goddamned ice. *Please* – *(He hangs up, catches himself.)* Shoot!

COBB. Almost – just a little slip-up right at the end.

CHARLIE. *(Starting to leave.)* I'll work on it.

> *(***COBB***: at the drinks table.)*

COBB. You had breakfast yet?

CHARLIE. No, sir, we came straight from the airport.

COBB. Breakfast is the most important meal of the day! Get over here. *(He hands* **CHARLIE** *a drink.)*

CHARLIE. Bourbon for breakfast?

COBB. What time is it in New York?

> *(***CHARLIE*** *checks his watch.)*

CHARLIE. Around noon.

COBB. *Lunch* is the most important meal of the day. Cheers!

> *(They drink.* **COBB** *sucks his down in one gulp;* **CHARLIE** *shakes his head after every tentative sip.)*

So? Where is he? I wanna meet him. My child prodigy?

CHARLIE. He's thirty-two, sir.

COBB. For what I'm paying? I'll bounce him on my knee, call him "sonny" if I like.

CHARLIE. It's your prerogative, sir.

COBB. If by "prerogative" you mean "pay check" then I couldn't agree more.

CHARLIE. He's um…in the hallway, sir. Resting.

COBB. Resting?

CHARLIE. On the luggage cart. Needed a little time.

COBB. Well, get him in here, what are we waitin' for? And next time, be more emphatic about the ice. I'm sure our guest will want ice with his brunch bourbon.

CHARLIE. I thought we were havin' lunch?

COBB. What time is it here?

CHARLIE. (*Checks his watch again.*) It's err…right about…

COBB.	**CHARLIE.**
(*Gleefully.*) The most *important* meal of the day!! Pour me another.	(*Simultaneously.*)…brunch time.

> (**CHARLIE** *pours another glass and then picks up the phone and yells into it.*)

CHARLIE. (*Into receiver.*) ICE, DAMMIT! AND I MEAN IT THIS TIME!!

> (*He slams it down really hard.*)

How's that?

COBB. Better. Now…usher in our guest.

> (*Beat.*)

CHARLIE. Mr. Cobb…before I bring him in…there's something I think you should know.

COBB. Yeah?

CHARLIE. Okay, think back:

COBB. Okay?

CHARLIE. To January:

COBB. All right.

CHARLIE. Remember the man you met in New York?

COBB. Sure.

CHARLIE. Confidently signing autographs at Sardi's, opening night. After his thrilling debut?

COBB. Yeah?

CHARLIE. The man who appeared to be on top of the

world – the toast of Broadway?

COBB. Charlie...?

CHARLIE. The man the critics fawned over, the man whose comic sensibility was so sublime you likened him to, to...

COBB. Molière, if I recall.

CHARLIE. The great Molière!

COBB. I told that half-wit from *The New York Times*, "Hey, half-wit, this guy's the next Molière...and you can quote me."

CHARLIE. And he *did* quote you.

COBB. *(Like it's a famous quote.)* "I am nothing if not quotable!"

CHARLIE. *(Beat.)* Who said that?

COBB. I did.

CHARLIE. *(He keeps on going.)* ...And on the strength of that first break-out smash-hit play you made this *astonishing offer*...this generous *invitation*. Put so much of your personal wealth...and personal integrity on the line. You remember that man?

COBB. Remember him? Charlie, I've invested every last nickel I ever made in this business in that guy. So go get him! *(As* **CHARLIE** *starts for the door...)* Whattayoo –? *Remember* him? I got my future, and *yours*, and several *others*, riding on the line here. The eggs are all in "the next Molière's" basket. Do I remember him? I *own* him. I hate him. But I *need* him. Because I need a play. A funny play. A *really* funny play. Or I'm done. If lightning doesn't strike *twice* – I'm gonna jump in the bathtub with a hair dryer, and do it myself.

CHARLIE. Okay, never mind.

COBB. G'head.

CHARLIE. Nope, nuthin'.

COBB. Charlie?

> *(He briefly opens the door, and then suddenly closes it.)*

CHARLIE. He seems somewhat...*different.*

COBB. Different?

CHARLIE. Somewhat.

COBB. You're makin' me nervous, Charlie.

CHARLIE. Sorry.

COBB. Your *job*...

CHARLIE. I know.

COBB. Your *primary* responsibility, need I remind you...?

CHARLIE. I know.

COBB. ...Is to *prevent* me from having a heart attack before I'm good and ready...

CHARLIE. I know, sir, but...

COBB. ...Is to *forestall* the inevitable stroke my doctor has "prescribed" for me at my annual check-up for the last twenty years.

CHARLIE. Prescribed? Don't you mean "predicted"?

COBB. Guy's *sadistic:* he wrote it down on a little piece of paper and stuck it in my shirt pocket. For twenty years! Can't read his handwriting, *but I know what it says!* Your job is to guarantee I have good days, even though on my calendar I've entered "bad day, bad day, bad day" the entire month of July!! So when you tell me my Golden Child is different...

CHARLIE. Sir, I...

COBB. When you say my Great Hope For The Future is *different.* I wanna know *how*, exactly. Different how? Spit it out!

CHARLIE. I don't think he's well, sir.

COBB. Like he's sick?

CHARLIE. I think so, sir.

COBB. Like jet lag?

> (**CHARLIE** *shakes his head "No" to each suggestion.*)

Like hungover?

Run down?

Like seasonal allergies?

What kinda sick?

CHARLIE. I would say...well, in my opinion...well, I think he's suffering from a touch of depression, sir.

COBB. Depression?

CHARLIE. Just a touch.

He's depressed. He's moody.

COBB. Moody and depressed?

CHARLIE. That's right.

COBB. He's a writer. They're all moody and depressed.

CHARLIE. Sir...

COBB. It's a horrible life. I wouldn't wish it on my worst enemy.

CHARLIE. It's a general kind of *malaise*... I think, he...

COBB. Malaise?

CHARLIE. Generally.

COBB. A general malaise.

CHARLIE. He said, in the car, that he was suffering from melancholy.

(Pause.)

COBB. "Melancholy"?

CHARLIE. Yup.

COBB. Melancholy/malaise? Are we talking food here, or sickness? I'm confused.

CHARLIE. It's a sickness, sir.

COBB. Melancholy?

*(**CHARLIE** nods.)*

That's actually a *thing*?

CHARLIE. For artists, yes.

COBB. Okay. And what causes it?

CHARLIE. Sir?

COBB. How do you get it? Melancholy.

CHARLIE. Err...

COBB. I got a doctor in Scottsdale...he'll write a prescription...get him on the phone, we'll get some pills, everything's hunky-dory.

CHARLIE. There's often no cause, sir.

COBB. No cause?

No *cause?*

CHARLIE. No.

COBB. It's just a thing you *get?*

For no reason? Whatsoever? And they got no pills for this? And there's nothing I can do? Even if I get *emphatic?*

CHARLIE. I think... I think...

COBB. And it's only writers who get this?

CHARLIE. Painters too, I imagine.

COBB. House painters?

CHARLIE. No *painter*-painters. Musicians, too. Dancers maybe.

COBB. But not you and me. Not *business* people?

CHARLIE. I don't think so sir.

COBB. Are we immune? To melancholy?

CHARLIE. I just think we're too busy.

COBB. Okay, look... Charlie. *(Beckoning to him.)* Here's what we're gonna do.

CHARLIE. *(Goes to him.)* Sir?

COBB. Not too close, it's hot.

> *(**CHARLIE** allows a respectful distance then.)*

We're gonna do nothin'.

CHARLIE. Nothing?

COBB. Write this down: "We do nothing." This has always been my strategy. When I have no clue what to do? I do *nothing.*

> *(**CHARLIE** has his little notepad out again.)*

CHARLIE. I think that's very wise, sir. *(Jotting it down.)* "Do nothing."

COBB. We're gonna pretend you never *said* what you just said.

CHARLIE. About the –

COBB. Zzzt, zzzt, zzt...

CHARLIE. Understand, sir. "We say *nothing*."

COBB. I mean, did he tell you to tell me this?

(**CHARLIE** *shakes his head, "No."*)

Did he say, "Please apologize to Mr. Cobb"?

(**CHARLIE** *shakes his head again.*)

Did he proffer: "He's paying me a shit-load of money to write him a script. I know he didn't bring me out here – all-expenses-paid – so I can sit under a palm tree with general malaise"?

(**CHARLIE** *laughs.*)

This is funny to you?

CHARLIE. No, it's just: every time you say "General Malaise" I picture a French guy in uniform.

COBB. This is not a joke!

CHARLIE. Sorry.

COBB. This is my livelihood, Charlie.

And *yours*.

And the other guy and the other guy and the other guy.

CHARLIE. Do I know those other guys?

COBB. They're silent partners.

Now focus: did he say anything of the kind?

CHARLIE. *(Focusing.)* No, sir.

COBB. Then if he didn't bring it up...we don't bring it up.

CHARLIE. We don't bring it up.

COBB. Nothin' is brought up. No talk of depression. No malaise, general or otherwise. And especially, no melancholy.

CHARLIE. "No melancholy."

COBB. Are you writing this down? If I hear the word "melancholy" in any context, we got trouble. Got it?

CHARLIE. Melancholy…should not be referred to…in any context. Got it.

COBB. Everything: business as usual. Everything: according to plan. Sparkle! *(Re:* **CHARLIE**'s *notepad.)* Now gimme that!

> *(***CHARLIE** *hands over his notepad.)*

What is this?

CHARLIE. What you told me to write.

COBB. And what does it say?

CHARLIE. "Say nothing. Do nothing."

COBB. And what would ya call that?

CHARLIE. Err…

COBB. It's called "evidence."

> *(He tears the sheet from the pad; crumples it up and hands it to* **CHARLIE**.*)*

You're gonna have to eat it, kid!

CHARLIE. Eat it?

COBB. Eat all trace of what I told you *what not* to do.

> *(***CHARLIE** *places it in his mouth and starts to chew.)*

CHARLIE. It's a little dry.

COBB. That's the lesson! *(Beat.)* Now, the clock is ticking.

> *(***COBB** *gestures grandly toward the door.)*

CHARLIE. *(Heading for the door.)* Okay, Mr. Cobb, consider yourself warned. Here he is, in all his glory…

> *(***CHARLIE** *goes out into the hallway.* **COBB** *wipes his brow with a handkerchief. There is a moment, and then* **DANNY** *a.k.a.* **"NEBRASKA" JONES** *enters the suite carrying a slim leather attaché, which he clutches tightly. He looks terrible. He looks like he slept in his clothes. He looks depressed.* **COBB** *embraces* **DANNY** *warmly.)*

There he is. Danny Jones.

DANNY. *(Glumly.)* I need a drink.

    (**CHARLIE** *is busy fixing* **DANNY**'s *drink.*)

COBB. Sorry – "*Nebraska*" Jones now, I guess.

DANNY. My agent's idea.

COBB. Terrific idea. Right, Charlie?

CHARLIE. I love it I love it I love it.

DANNY. I'm depressed I need a drink.

COBB. *(Covering.)* Great name for a great writer.
    And – if you don't mind – um...why "Nebraska"?

DANNY. Tennessee was taken.

COBB. No, I mean...how'd you settle on the nickname "Nebraska"?

DANNY. My folks.

COBB. Yeah?

DANNY. Had sex in a hotel.

COBB. Oh.

DANNY. In Cincinnati.
    Where I was conceived.

CHARLIE. *(Handing him a tumbler of bourbon.)* But Nebraska's nowhere near Cincinnati.

DANNY. They missed their connection.
    They *shoulda* been having sex in Omaha.

    (**DANNY** *takes a sip. Then, rather philosophically:*)

Bourbon. I love bourbon. It is a comfort to me.

COBB. And there's plenty more where that came from.

CHARLIE. Two cases.

COBB. Two cases.

CHARLIE. With his name on 'em.

COBB. With your name on 'em. Whatever you need, Danny. Whatever your heart's desire. You just ask.

    (**DANNY** *sniffs, looks at his glass.*)

DANNY. No ice?

COBB. Here, take mine.

DANNY. – Err…

COBB. It's an honor, please. I insist.

> *(In one quick move,* **COBB** *drains his glass of bourbon, takes* **DANNY**'s *drink, and pours it into his own ice-filled glass.* **COBB** *sees from* **DANNY**'s *reaction that he must now quickly spin a reasonable anthropological justification for his breach of etiquette.)*

There is a long-standing tradition…amongst my people…to offer our honored guests ice from the first drink we share together under the same roof.

DANNY. Who's your people?

COBB. The Thirteenth Tribe of Israel.

DANNY. I thought there were only twelve.

COBB. It's a religion shrouded in mystery. *L'Chaim!*

> *(***DANNY*** drinks.* **COBB** *shoots* **CHARLIE** *a glance.)*

(Sotto voce.) Ice!

> *(***CHARLIE*** heads for the door.)*

CHARLIE. Did um…did the airline lose your luggage, Mr. Jones? I only see the one bag.

DANNY. There is only one bag.

CHARLIE. Traveling light, huh?

DANNY. When I'm sick I don't change.

COBB. What?

DANNY. When I'm sick, I have no need of additional garments.

> *(***COBB*** and* **CHARLIE** *exchange panicked looks.)*

COBB. You don't look, sick, Danny.

CHARLIE. No…getouttahere!

COBB. You look the picture of good health. Isn't that right, Charlie?

DANNY. Really? Because I feel –

CHARLIE. Fit as a fiddle!

You could be on the cover of *All-American Athlete.*

DANNY. I'm a playwright.

CHARLIE. And if they had a magazine for robust and physically fit playwrights...with well-defined fingers...you'd be on that cover *too*.

COBB. Don't worry about clothes. We'll get you something. In a light linen. You look to me to be about a 44-Long?*

DANNY. When I'm sick I get down to a 39.**

COBB. *(Sotto voce, to CHARLIE.)* Get him a 39, tear out the tag, sew in a new tag.

CHARLIE. 44-Long?

COBB. Atta boy!

You hungry, Danny?

DANNY. Couldn't touch a thing.

COBB. We got your favorite.

> *(COBB pulls the lid off the tray to reveal the sandwich.)*

Roast beef.

DANNY. Did they slice it thin? If it's not paper-thin I can't touch it.

> *(COBB glares at CHARLIE.)*

I like to be able see through my beef.

> *(CHARLIE has surreptitiously taken the roast beef from the sandwich and is attempting to scrape off the mustard and carefully stretch out the beef – he checks to see if he can see daylight through it.)*

CHARLIE. Looks delicious! And transparent.

DANNY. On second thought, I don't have much of an appetite. And I can't help noticing, it's a little warm in here. Isn't it?

COBB. Warm? I don't know, is it warm?

Does it feel warm to you, Charlie?

---

* Or whatever size the actor playing Danny would wear.
** Several sizes *smaller* than whatever size the actor playing Danny would wear.

CHARLIE. *(Already heading for the door.)* Not really, but I'm working on it.

(**CHARLIE** *exits the hotel room.*)

DANNY. The air feels...

COBB. What?

DANNY. Maybe it's just me, but...

COBB. Speak freely.

DANNY. The air in here feels somewhat...

COBB. Charged?

DANNY. I was gonna say "swampy."

COBB. No, no, it's *charged,* alright. *(He walks* **DANNY** *over to the couch.)* The atmosphere must sense your presence, Danny.

(**DANNY** *laughs obligingly.*)

No, I'm serious. Your words...you think I'm kidding? You have a very special gift. When I saw your play...

DANNY. Oh you made it?

COBB. I made it *eleven* times...

DANNY. Wow! Eleven?

COBB. ...and every time was an epiphany...*and* a revelation...hand to God! I had to stop going because I couldn't handle that many epiphanies and revelations so close together. Those characters...those words... what those people *said*...and *did*... *(He has no idea what he's talking about.)* ...on that *stage.* Such peaks, such valleys. *Electrifying*'s the only word that comes close.

DANNY. What was your favorite part?

COBB. My favorite part...?

DANNY. I mean I have my favorites, but I'm curious...from an outside observer, a Broadway veteran like yourself.

COBB. My favorite *part.*

DANNY. If you don't mind.

COBB. Whhheeewww! It's hard to pick. There's so much to choose from. Between all those epiphanies and revelations. But, if I had to...

DANNY. Yeah?

COBB. If there was a gun to my head.

DANNY. Indulge me.

COBB. Well... I would have to say... I'm partial to the bit where...the, the main character...

DANNY. Florence.

COBB. Where Florence...does that *thing*...where she...

DANNY. Oh, I know...

COBB. She, she...ah, what's the word...

DANNY. "Talks" to?

COBB. Talks to the...guy? The...the...

DANNY. Which one, which scene, the priest or the fireman?

COBB. Well *both*, but the priest...

DANNY. Yeah.

COBB. I mean, come on, Danny...the scene with the priest is so...what??

DANNY. Confessional.

COBB. There you go. Yes. It's *extremely* confessional. It's probably the most confessional thing I've seen on Broadway in years. You said it better than I ever could.

DANNY. Can I ask you? Did you believe it? The confession?

COBB. *(Nervous he'll be caught out.)* You know? I don't think it matters. In my heart... I don't think it matters whether we believe the confession or not...because the confession...the nature of the *confession* Danny...well, it's...it's sacred isn't it.

DANNY. It *is* sacred.

COBB. It was offered in confidence, so who am I? "*Secreto del silencio.*" Huh? Who are you? Who is *anybody* to question...?

DANNY. Right!

COBB. To question his veracity –

DANNY. Her veracity –

COBB. – Her veracity.
Period.

(**COBB** *throws up his hands in the air.*)

COBB. *(Cont.)* I have nothing more to say.

> (*Silence. They both just look at each other nodding. Then* **DANNY** *embraces him passionately.*)

DANNY. That's very kind of you, Mr. Cobb. Thank you.

COBB. No, thank *you*.

For *being* here.

At my invitation.

To work on something new.

Something that's gonna eclipse anything *anybody* has *ever* seen on *any* stage, *anywhere*, at *any* time, in the *history* of the theatre.

DANNY. That's…quite a lot of hype. And a lot of pressure.

COBB. I have faith.

Danny Nebraska Jones:

I can't tell ya…how thrilled, how honored, *humbled*… how immeasurably happy I am that you're here.

DANNY. *(Sullenly.)* Happy?

COBB. My joy knows no bounds.

DANNY. *(Sighs.)* Wish I was happy.

COBB. And yet… I am also realistic. Just to, just to… *(Keeps going.)* If I can contribute in some small way to your genius, your artistry. *Whooooofff*, that's something…I'll remember the rest of my life. If I haven't said it: I love writers! *(Pause.)* Now… I'm gonna get outta your hair. Relax. *(Re: the attaché.)* Can I take that from ya?

> (**DANNY** *recoils violently as* **CHARLIE** *attempts to relieve him of his attaché.*)

DANNY. Those are my notes! I don't like to share my notes. They're sacred.

COBB. Yes, of course. Hands off, sacred. Believe you me. There's a safe in the bedroom.

You are my guest here. Anything you want. This room… it's yours…in perpetuity. No pressure. Whenever the muse strikes. *(A little joke; he can't help himself.)* If it strikes. I'm not worried! And when it does... I want you to be ready. "The readiness is all." Now...what can I get you? Your wish is my command.

DANNY. Can I have another drink?

> *(**CHARLIE** bursts through the door so fast that a couple cubes skitter out of the ice bucket he's carrying. He heads for the bar.)*

CHARLIE. Ice, I got ice.

COBB. Charlie!

CHARLIE. I was emphatic.

DANNY. I'm thirsty.

COBB. Nebraska Jones is thirsty.

> *(**CHARLIE** fills a bar glass with ice for **DANNY**, but...)*

DANNY. And uh...is there anything we can do about the A/C?

COBB. I don't know. Charlie? Is there anything we can do about the A/C?

DANNY. Like fixing it?

> *(...**DANNY** has taken the filled ice bucket across the room with a bottle of bourbon and proceeds to pour the entire contents into the bucket. They watch him with horror. When the ice bucket is full of booze, **CHARLIE** accommodates him by placing a straw and a little umbrella in **DANNY**'s massive drink.)*

CHARLIE. It's next on my list of emphatic things to do.

DANNY. Or switching rooms?

CHARLIE. They're overbooked.

COBB. Don't you worry, Charlie's on it. It'll get fixed. Kid's a terrier! You got things to think about. Last thing we want you worrying about is sweat. *(Heading for the TV.)* Let's watch *Lassie*. You like *Lassie*? It's my favorite. *(Snaps his fingers at **CHARLIE**.)*

(**CHARLIE** *switches on the TV for a second and we hear Lassie barking. They stand and stare at the TV – from the sound of it, it's an episode in which Lassie gets caught in a bear trap, or something, because Lassie is whining in pain. Beat. They are momentarily transfixed, then* **DANNY** *heads off to put his attaché in the hotel room safe. He is briefly offstage, but the dialogue continues through the following exchange.*)

DANNY. *(Offstage.)* When I'm depressed I don't sweat.

COBB. You don't sweat?

DANNY. *(Offstage.)* Not when I'm depressed.

(**COBB** *snaps his finger again;* **CHARLIE** *switches off the TV.*)

COBB. You're not depressed.

DANNY. *(Offstage.)* I'm a little depressed.

CHARLIE. You can't be depressed.

DANNY. *(Offstage.)* I'm moody and depressed. All my pores have contracted and clogged.

(**DANNY** *returns to the stage, looking pitiful.*)

I'm moody and depressed and contracted and clogged.

COBB. No, no, actually I think I see a few beads glistening right there on your forehead.

CHARLIE. I see 'em, too.

DANNY. You do?

COBB. Oh, sure, your whole forehead is shining.

DANNY. I'm sweating?

COBB. I'm sweating. You're sweating. Everybody's sweating.

DANNY. That's a good sign, I guess.

COBB. It's a terrific sign. Look at that, Charlie, he's sweating. Are you sweating, Charlie?

CHARLIE. Rivers, boss.

COBB. *Rivers* the man is sweating. You see? We're all sweating. You know why? Because this is Arizona. We're in a desert. And we're not depressed. It's just plain hot. You know the phrase: "Never let 'em see ya sweat"?

DANNY. Uh-huh?

COBB. Well, they don't have that here. Here they got: "*Always* let 'em see you sweat." Or else you're dead. You know, because of the cooling effect... *(He moves his hands around in circles in lieu of knowing exactly the point he is trying to make.)* They should make it the state slogan: "Arizona, boy do we sweat!"

DANNY. It's not the heat I mind so much. I just like the hum of the air conditioner.

COBB. You like the hum?

DANNY. Helps me sleep.

COBB. And sleep you shall. Charlie? He likes the hum.

DANNY. Good, because...actually... I'm tired... I'm bordering on groggy.

COBB. *(Doesn't like where this is heading.)* Groggy?

DANNY. And I usually only get tired, when I'm...

COBB. Zzzt, zzzt, zzt...

DANNY. You know, maybe I'm...

COBB. Or maybe not.

DANNY. ...I think perhaps...

CHARLIE. Or don't think.

DANNY. ...that I might just be...

COBB. Forget it.

DANNY. ...I'm coming down with...

CHARLIE. Jet lag.

DANNY. With a case of...

COBB. Seasonal allergies.

DANNY. Melancholy.

> *(Dead silence. **COBB** and **CHARLIE** stand absolutely frozen, like statues. Then... **CHARLIE** begins to hum!)*

CHARLIE. Mmmmmmmmmmmm...!!

DANNY. I'm sorry Mr. Cobb… But when I'm melancholy…

COBB. *(Running interference.)* No one's saying you are. We don't even know what that is.

CHARLIE. Never heard of it – Mmmmmmm…

COBB. We don't got that in Arizona.

CHARLIE. In any context.

COBB. Melancholy. *(An idea.)* It's food, right? Somethin' your mother used to make.

> *(CHARLIE stops humming.)*

We'll get Chef Antoine on it right away – he's Michelin rated! Whattawee need, some melons? Some cauliflower? Bingo: *melancholy!*

DANNY. It's a serious form of depression, Mr. Cobb. Hamlet had it.

> *(COBB buries his face in his hands at the mention of Hamlet.)*

And when I'm melancholy…my bio-rhythms get all out of whack. I don't sweat, I don't eat, I can't watch TV, I don't write.

COBB. Wait! – What was that last thing?

DANNY. I don't write. My fingers rebel – becoming fat and cumbersome – useless stubby sausages. Depression is a horrible thing, Mr. Cobb.

COBB. Can we get a second opinion?

DANNY. All you wanna do is sleep. And drink.

COBB. *(Feeling nauseous.)* And you don't write?

DANNY. How can I? I stay in bed all day. And drink. I mean, in fairness, I also drink when I'm *not* depressed. But when I'm depressed, I mean I *drink…really* drink. Like…*drink*-drink.

COBB. *(Sotto voce, handing CHARLIE a bottle.)* Water it down. Water it all down!

> *(CHARLIE grabs an armful of bottles from the drinks table and staggers toward the door.)*

DANNY. *(Heading toward bedroom.)* I think I'll lie down for a few minutes. Leaf through a book, or somethin'.

> *(**CHARLIE** hears his cue and struggles into bedroom. He returns seconds later with a copy of* The Agony and the Ecstasy.*)*

COBB. A book? A book? We gotta book. Your favorite book.

CHARLIE. A first edition...of your favorite book –

> *(**COBB** takes the book from **CHARLIE** and tears it in half right down the spine.)*

COBB. Keep "The Agony" give 'em "The Ecstasy."

CHARLIE. The best *half* of your favorite book.

DANNY. Gee, thanks. I'll take a load off now. Maybe I'm just tired from the trip.

COBB. You go right ahead. The mattresses at this joint – like sleepin' on a cloud. The pillows soft as baby angels...with gossamer wings wafting you with a cool, cool heavenly breeze.

CHARLIE. *(Sotto voce, to **COBB**.)* That sounds depressing actually.

COBB. G'head, Danny. You're gonna wake up feeling like a million bucks.

> *(**DANNY** finally exits. **COBB** turns to **CHARLIE** with menace.)*

Sonofabitch *better* wake up feeling like a million bucks!

> *(He takes one last pull from a bottle of bourbon in **CHARLIE***'s arms.)*

Now, look, Charlie. *(Exhales audibly.)* I'm not saying you're not up to the challenge...but you got your work cut out for you. You've got until sunrise tomorrow to figure out why this schmuck is so depressed...figure out how to turn him around...guarantee tomorrow is a very good day for me, even if I'm scheduled for a bad one... get this damned air conditioning fixed or get us a new room.

> *(**CHARLIE** starts out.)*

COBB. *(Cont.)* And *Charlie?* I cannot express myself more clearly...

CHARLIE. *(Weakly.)* Be emphatic??

    (Blackout.)

Scene Two

(The same hotel room. It is the following morning around ten o'clock. The room is just as we left it – except the large overhead fan is now spinning at great velocity. There is kind of a "whooshing" sound in the air, an arctic wind. It's clear the A/C has been "fixed.")

(AT RISE: A mirror image of the play's opening – but instead of tossing a sofa cushion up into the fan blades to encourage them to start moving, this time **COBB** *– blue with cold – is trying to get the fan to stop, at any cost. He is just about to throw the pillow skyward, as...* **CHARLIE** *flies through the main door with a silver tray containing a small pot of coffee and a single cup and saucer. He is now wearing gloves, a scarf, and a knit hat.)*

CHARLIE. Don't do it, sir! You'll break a window.

COBB. Get it to stop, Charlie, for the love of God, get it to stop.

CHARLIE. They don't know how!

COBB. They don't know how?

CHARLIE. They've called in the experts, and they don't know how.

COBB. The entire heating and cooling staff of the Royal Palms Hotel *doesn't know how*??

CHARLIE. They have their theories.

COBB. What kind of theories?

CHARLIE. You sure you wanna know? I know talk of politics can put you in a bad mood.

COBB. How is air conditioning and overhead fans political?

CHARLIE. *(If you really want to hear.)* Well...the ventilation system at the hotel dates back to the twenties.

COBB. Okay.

CHARLIE. And the air conditioning was installed in the forties.

COBB. Go on.

CHARLIE. But a lot of the duct-work was modified in the fifties.

COBB. Uh-huh.

CHARLIE. With major upgrades done in the sixties.

COBB. Is this an excuse or a history lesson?

CHARLIE. The prevailing theory…

COBB. From the proletariat or the bourgeoisie?

CHARLIE. The prevailing theory is that what we got on our hands…

COBB. Yeah?

CHARLIE. With the extreme warm front, on one side… And the extreme cold front, on the other…

COBB. Yeah?

CHARLIE. Can only be described – in plumbing terminology – as a coup d'état!

COBB. For Chrissakes, Charlie!

CHARLIE. I told you it would upset you.

COBB. We're talkin' climate control, not geo-politics.

CHARLIE. The front desk seems to think it's the same thing. *(Beat.)* Like I said, it's just a theory.

COBB. Look up there…into the eye of the storm…weather like this shouldn't be happening in…

CHARLIE. Arizona?

COBB. *Indoors!*

I've done productions of *The Tempest* that weren't this realistic.

CHARLIE. Gimme the pillow.

> (**COBB** *hands over the pillow reluctantly. He pulls his collar up around his ears, blows into his hands, and stamps his feet.*)

COBB. What could possibly account for the malfunction with the A/C?

CHARLIE. You want my opinion?

COBB. G'head.

CHARLIE. We complained.

COBB. We complained?

CHARLIE. We complained *emphatically*.

We complained emphatically and they fixed it.

COBB. This is fixed?

CHARLIE. They said they fixed it *emphatically*.

COBB. It's subzero temperatures in here.

CHARLIE. Ain't that what we asked for…in a very emphatic way? *(Heading to the balcony window.)* I'll open the windows; it might warm up the place. Equalize things, ya know?

COBB. I already tried. The handle snapped off from metal fatigue. Thing's frozen shut.

> *(Beat.)*

We're gonna die in here, Charlie, you know that? My obituary will read: "Mr. Jerry M. Cobb, Jr. of Flushing, New York, froze to death yesterday afternoon. Cause of death: business trip to Scottsdale."

CHARLIE. I'll call down again. See if I can get 'em to recalibrate.

> *(**CHARLIE** picks up the hotel phone.)*

COBB. Obb-bubb-bub-bub-buh! Be very careful what you say, Charlie. The global climate depends on it.

> *(**CHARLIE** takes a slow, deep breath in…and out to calm his nerves before placing the call.)*

CHARLIE. *(Into phone receiver, very calmly.)* This is Charlie Bascher in 306, calling on behalf of Mr. Jerry Cobb.

COBB. The *late* Jerry Cobb.

CHARLIE. *(Into phone.)* I know, yeah… *(Rolls eyes.)* Thanks for fixing it…but you fixed it too much!

COBB. Unfix it a little!

CHARLIE. *(Into phone.)* Can you unfix it a little?

> *(Pause.)*

CHARLIE. *(Cont.)* Uh-huh? Uh-huh? Uh-huh?

COBB. What he say?

CHARLIE. Not without the paperwork.

COBB. Okay, ask him: what's he get paid an hour?

CHARLIE. *(Into phone.)* What's your hourly wage, pal? Uh-huh.

COBB. And what are we paying for this room?

CHARLIE. *(Into phone.)* Do you know what these rooms go for?

Uh-huh? Uh-huh? Uh-huh?

COBB. What he say?

CHARLIE. Not without the paperwork.

COBB. This country, I swear!

CHARLIE. *(Still on the line.)* No, I appreciate that, but is there any way to adjust it? *(He listens.)* Can I what? Describe it? The current atmospheric conditions? *(He looks at* **COBB**, *who is blowing on his hands.)* Well, Mr. Cobb said: yesterday was the "Ninth Circle of Hell." And today?

COBB. *(Shivering.)* "Ten steps from the Pole."

CHARLIE. *(Into phone.)* Ya hear that?

COBB. *(More to himself.)* Now I know how Shackleton felt.

CHARLIE. *(Into phone.)* Well, thanks for all your help. *(He hangs up.)* He's going to try and recalibrate.

COBB. Great. *(His hands: scales.)* Siberian Winter or Tropic of Cancer. The suspense is killing me.

CHARLIE. For now he says, "Jiggle the handle."

COBB. "Jiggle the handle"? This is his expert advice?

> *(***COBB*** "jiggles" the control for the overhead fan. It breaks off in his hand.)*

CHARLIE. Did it help?

> *(The fan is beginning to slow and comes to a standstill.)*

COBB. It cut the "wind-chill" factor. But I still can't feel my toes...or whatever those *things* are at the end of the things I *think* are my feet.

CHARLIE. Here... I was an Eagle Scout.

> (**CHARLIE** *unzips a couple of cushions from the sofa and helps* **COBB** *to stick them onto his feet – an extra layer of protection.*)

COBB. *(Mildly impressed.)* They got a merit badge for every-thing! *(He notices the tray.)* Hey, is that coffee?

CHARLIE. Fresh from the pot. Piping hot.

COBB. Is there sugar?

CHARLIE. Three lumps – just the way you like it.

COBB. You're a life-saver!

CHARLIE. *(Points.)* There's a spoon in the cup, all you gotta do is stir.

> (**COBB** *grabs the spoon and stirs, only to discover the coffee has frozen solid in the cup like a coffee popsicle. He lifts the brown clump right out of the cup and gestures to* **CHARLIE**.)

COBB. I'd laugh if I didn't think my teeth'd fall out.

CHARLIE. I guess you gotta drink it fast.

COBB. I'd cry, but I don't want my eyeballs to frost over.

CHARLIE. I'll get more, sir.

COBB. Get a pot. A great big pot!

CHARLIE. Yes, sir.

COBB. And a hair dryer.

> *(Beat.* **COBB** *drifts over to the bedroom door and peers in.)*

CHARLIE. How's he look?

COBB. You know the phrase "return on investment"?

CHARLIE. Yeah?

COBB. Not like that. *(Pause.)* Listen, I want him alert when he finally stirs. We've got work to do. Did you hear him last night?

CHARLIE. I know.

COBB. All he's got is *notes*. I didn't pay for notes: I paid for a masterpiece. *(A Zen thing.)* I'm not gonna let this little hiccup get in the way. We've already wasted a day with General Malaise.

> *(**CHARLIE** laughs.)*

All right, cut it out.

CHARLIE. Sorry sir.

COBB. We can't stay here forever. I'm not made of money. When I leave Arizona I can't be saddled with a stack of bills *this* high. *(He gestures.)* Bar bills, hotel bills, medical bills.

CHARLIE. *(Confused.)* Medical bills?

COBB. For the frostbite!

CHARLIE. I thought it was heat stroke?

COBB. Which *progressed* to frostbite.

CHARLIE. Didn't we promise him the room…in perpetuity?

COBB. I was being hyperbolic. That's always been my strategy.

CHARLIE. Hyperbole?

COBB. *Lying.* I'm a producer – it's a reflex.

CHARLIE. "The truth will set you free." Isn't that what they say?

COBB. Who says? Do you *know* who says?

CHARLIE. I dunno, sir.

COBB. Me either, but it's probably not a producer – so don't give me advice I can't use.

CHARLIE. Mr. Cobb? Can I ask you a question?

COBB. G'head.

CHARLIE. Is this a good day or a bad day so far?

COBB. What do you think?

> *(Beat.)*

CHARLIE. I'll get that coffee now.

COBB. Wait! First things first: you need to get me the combination to that safe.

CHARLIE. Sir, I have to object. This man is a guest of the hotel and as such, he must be provided the utmost protection when it comes to his personal effects.

COBB. Judas!

CHARLIE. Just kidding. Got it right here.

> (**CHARLIE** *shoots his cuff and holds up the back of his hand.*)

COBB. You had me fooled for a second, Charlie. Wrote it on the back of your hand, huh? – Quick thinking!

CHARLIE. Thought it might come in handy.

COBB. I need to take a look at his notes – see what he's got. Review the premise. Make sure we're on the right track.

CHARLIE. Got it.

COBB. I'd rather be *braced* for disappointment than surprised by it.

CHARLIE. Is that another one of your strategies?

COBB. No, I learned it from my ex-wife.

> *(Beat.)*

And this, Charlie...come here... *(He pulls him in close.)* ...this is of particular interest and importance to me.

CHARLIE. *(Vaguely uncomfortable.)* Why are you holding me so close, sir?

COBB. You're warm. *(Beat.)* Charlie... I need you to figure out why Danny Nebraska Jones is feeling so...

CHARLIE. Zzzt, zzzt, zzt...

COBB. *(Catches himself.)* So... Blue.

CHARLIE. *(Revealing back of other hand.)* Already done, sir. Got it right here.

COBB. What is that?

CHARLIE. I did some sleuthing around after you went to bed.

COBB. Ambition never sleeps.

CHARLIE. It turns out Danny's got a fiancée.

COBB. Why's that depressing?

CHARLIE. Turns out she left him.

COBB. Why'd she leave?

CHARLIE. Turns out she's an actress.
With *ambition*.

COBB. Interesting.

CHARLIE. Turns out she just got offered a part in a new play in Sacramento, California. Turns out she was *miffed* she never got a part in his hit play in New York.

COBB. Turns out you've solved our problem, Charlie. I won't forget this.

CHARLIE. Thank you, sir, I won't let you.

COBB. I want that woman on the next flight from Sacramento.

CHARLIE. Done.

COBB. And I don't care if she arrives kickin' and screamin'. She wants to be a star? – Promise her this: *this* is the new play she's been waiting for; *this* is her ticket; her star vehicle; meteoric; it's gonna be the funniest thing to hit Broadway since, since...

CHARLIE. Is this hyperbole again?

COBB. It's gonna be a masterpiece. Ain't that what the critics want? A "masterpiece of comic timing"? In fact... *(He claps his hands together.)* ...that's what we're gonna call it!

CHARLIE. Are you sure?

COBB. I'm positive.
What?

CHARLIE. No, it's just that...

COBB. What, that *what?*

CHARLIE. 'S a little risky is all.

COBB. Risky?

CHARLIE. Well, because...what if it's...

COBB. What? What are you driving at Charlie?

CHARLIE. You're actually gonna call the play *A Masterpiece* *of Comic Timing?*

COBB. If the critics can sling shit around, why can't we? "The best movie of the year!" and it's January 4!

CHARLIE. But, sir...

COBB. It's a good title, don't you think? It'll sell tickets.

CHARLIE. It'll sell tickets...it'll sell a few tickets until...

COBB. Until what??

CHARLIE. Mr. Cobb what if it's not...

COBB. Not what?

CHARLIE. ...a masterpiece? What if it's...what if it's not... *funny.*

> (**COBB** *chuckles to himself. He slaps* **CHARLIE** *on the back warmly.*)

COBB. Charlie, Charlie, Charlie. I love you kid. And I envy you...your naïveté. You're worried it won't be a masterpiece?

CHARLIE. You don't know. It's presumptive.

COBB. You worry it won't be funny?

CHARLIE. You can't predict what audiences will laugh at. Or what they'll like. How they'll respond. They're mercurial. They're fickle. They're lemmings...

COBB. Lemmings?

CHARLIE. ...leaping off the same cliff of popularity.

COBB. Oh is that what they are?

CHARLIE. You can't be that presumptuous, Mr. Cobb, you can't be *arrogant,* sir...so conceited that you call your own play *A Masterpiece* of *Comic Timing!!* You're setting yourself up for disaster! You're just sticking your neck out...asking the critics to chop off your head with a byline that reads: "It didn't live up to its name!!"

> (*Silence.*)

COBB. Charlie Bascher.

Look at me.

I'm gonna tell you something.

(Beat.)

COBB. *(Cont.)* All the years I been in this business, I picked up a trick or two, and now I'm gonna share a sliver of my considerable wisdom, because I think you deserve to hear it... I think you're *ready.*

CHARLIE. For what, sir?

COBB. The truth.

The theatrical truth.

The God's Honest Theatrical Truth!

(Pause.)

The audience...

CHARLIE. Uh-huh?

COBB. Is smarter than you are.

CHARLIE. I did pretty good in school.

COBB. But the *audience* doesn't care if it's a masterpiece.

CHARLIE. They don't?

COBB. The *audience*...is just happy to get out of the house...

CHARLIE. But, sir...

COBB. The audience...doesn't *know* if it's a masterpiece.

CHARLIE. How come?

COBB. Because the audience has surrendered its independent will for something infinitely more valuable...a *group* experience, a "collective unconscious..."

CHARLIE. *(With notebook at the ready.)* Should I be writing this down?

COBB. Of course.

CHARLIE. Are ya gonna make me eat it?

COBB. Whattsamatter?

CHARLIE. I had a big breakfast.

COBB. *(Ignoring him and continuing.)* Individually, each audience member could be a genius – but you clump 'em all together, not so much. You could have an audience of Einsteins. Four hundred Einsteins all sitting out there in the audience –

CHARLIE. But you're saying that collectively they're dumb? A room full of Einsteins is dumb?

COBB. No, a room full of Einsteins is smart, but wants something different. The audience wishes to be "as one."

CHARLIE. As one "what," sir?

I'm not following the math. Four-hundred Einsteins...

COBB. It's a metaphor, doesn't matter. Once they pay their money – they feel it.

CHARLIE. As one?

COBB. *(Nodding.)* It's really the only reason to go to the theatre...so you can, for a little while no longer be burdened with your own individual problems...your bullshit...your demons...your petty bourgeois headaches. Your *laundry*. But *instead* be absorbed...hell *exalted* by the collective joyful experience of being part of the *Human Race*, not a person, a singular dot.

CHARLIE. *(Repeating the lesson he thinks he's learned.)* I go to the theatre to *not* feel like Einstein.

COBB. The audience wants to be released from the responsibility of "*taste*" – they don't want to have to decide what's good and what's bad...they want to be *told*... and will feel let down if we fail to do so. *(Beat.)* If they are told in the right way, then it *will* be right...and it will be true...but the elixir is only potent if we *tell* 'em, Charlie. We can't ask 'em...we gotta tell 'em.

It's our job to tell 'em.

CHARLIE. And we're *gonna* tell 'em?

COBB. Baby, we're gonna *proclaim* it.

See: the audience doesn't know what's funny.

The audience needs to be *told* what's funny.

How else you gonna get four-hundred Einsteins to agree what's funny? To laugh at the same instant?

(Beat.)

CHARLIE. I believe you?

COBB. The audience will laugh at those moments we

sensitively *engineer* to provoke their laughter.

CHARLIE. But, but…

COBB. They will cry when we need them to cry. And they will be rapt when we need them to be rapt.

CHARLIE. Wrapped in what?

COBB. Rapt with attention. Because the words, Charlie… just the words…the words will be placed…in precisely the right order.

CHARLIE. They will?

COBB. As to demonstrate…

CHARLIE. Uh-huh.

COBB. …to the audience…

CHARLIE. Uh-huh.

COBB. …both the *mastery*…and the comic brilliance of our play.

> *(Beat.)*

CHARLIE. And what if you're wrong?

COBB. Then we're *fucked* and I lose a million dollars!! Now go find this dame.

And you tell her that. Tell her *all* of that.

CHARLIE. The Einsteins, the every –

COBB. The whole *schmear*. And you get her back here, as fast as you possibly can. What's her name?

> *(CHARLIE shoots his cuff and shows COBB the back of his hand. COBB reads:)*

22-36-28. *(Beat.)* You already got her measurements?

CHARLIE. Sorry, that's the combination to the safe.

> *(Shoots his other cuff and shows the back of his hand.)*

COBB. Nola Hart. Can't wait to meet her. Now get me those notes. And keep workin' on the weather.

> *(CHARLIE exits. COBB crosses to the table, where the sandwich from the previous scene is still under wraps. He's hungry, but can he really eat it? He*

stabs a knife into the sandwich and picks it up like a popsicle. He licks it. It ain't bad.)

(Blackout.)

Scene Three

(It is the next morning, just past noon.)

(AT RISE: **COBB** *is sitting on the sofa, the notes from* **DANNY**'*s attaché spread out before him on the coffee table.* **DANNY** *is sitting sullenly in an armchair, his teeth chattering, a wool blanket wrapped around him to fend off the cold, and a seat cushion unzipped and covering his head like a ski hat.)*

*(*ENTITY**CHARLIE** *has a large silver coffee pot and cups on a little serving table, and is using a blow dryer to keep the coffee hot. He's now wearing a long trench coat.)*

DANNY. I cannot believe you ransacked my room.

CHARLIE. We didn't ransack.

DANNY. I cannot believe you broke into my safe.

COBB. We had the combination.

DANNY. And pilfered my personal possessions.

COBB. You had six typed pages and a stale cheese sandwich in your attaché. That was the extent of your personal possessions.

DANNY. I can't *believe* you read my notes. It's a gross violation of privacy.

COBB. I paid for these notes. For the exclusive privilege of grossly violating your privacy. Paid *a lot*, if you recall.

DANNY. That doesn't give you the right to steal –

CHARLIE. We didn't steal, we *liberated.*

DANNY. These are *sacred* notes.

COBB. What's so sacred about 'em?

DANNY. I'm not gonna explain myself to a, a… Philistine.

COBB. That's the nicest thing anyone's ever said to me. Too bad I don't know what it means…or care.

DANNY. To an artist, some things are sacred. You wouldn't understand.

CHARLIE. *(Becoming increasingly emphatic.)* Oh, we understand. Like bourbon? We understand that's sacred. Like sleeping past noon? Like shirking responsibility for the work you were paid handsomely to do...because you feel down in the dumps!

COBB. Bubb-bubb-bubb!

CHARLIE. Like *feigning* melancholy.

DANNY. You can't feign melancholy.

CHARLIE. But apparently you can *drink it*!!

> *(***COBB*** crosses to **CHARLIE** to calm him down.)*

COBB. Charlie, take it easy. I like the new emphatic you, but...just take it easy. You okay? You don't look so good.

CHARLIE. I'm sorry, I'm just tired, Mr. Cobb. Ambition never sleeps!

> *(***COBB*** inspects several empty bottles on the drinks table.)*

COBB. Looks like you had quite the night, Danny. How many bottles did you go through?

DANNY. I don't remember.

CHARLIE. Three bottles. Three *whole* bottles.

DANNY. Impossible. I would be dead by now.

CHARLIE. Except I watered them down!!

COBB. Easy, Charlie. I'm glad Mr. Jones made himself at home. But now we got work to do, huh?

DANNY. Jerry...can I please get a change of clothes? I sweated clean through my suit *yesterday*...and today I think I've developed *permafrost*. I could really use a shower, a shave...it'll perk me right up.

CHARLIE. The plumbing, at present, is not functional. The shower heads are frozen. Glaciers have formed in the toilet bowl. And we're expecting two inches of precipitation in the bedroom.

> *(***CHARLIE*** is inspecting the air vents around the room. He has one of those small, two-or-three rung

*stepladders. As he climbs up on the step unit, he
begins to groan and swoon.* **COBB** *looks at him.)*

COBB. Whatsamatter kid?

CHARLIE. I have an acute form of vertigo.

COBB. You're two feet off the ground!

CHARLIE. That's what so acute about it.

*(He climbs down and moves the ladder to the next
air vent.)*

I talked to the Head of Maintenance.

COBB. And?

CHARLIE. He thinks they've figured out how to regulate the
temperature. He did warn me, for a while it could get
tempestuous. They're gonna reroute some duct-work
in the basement – change the general *gulf-stream* of the
building. We should be able to feel the effects within
the hour.

DANNY. *(To* **COBB**.*)* You promised to procure a new suit – a
linen suit.

COBB. I'm not procuring nothin' until we make some
headway, here, pal. Now fair's fair.

DANNY. Well, can I at least get some proper protection
from the cold? *(Points to the vent* **CHARLIE** *is right now
adjusting.)* There's a Nor'easter coming right out of
that vent. Do you have any ear muffs?

CHARLIE. Ears muffs? You have any idea how hard it would
be to procure ear muffs in Arizona in July?

COBB. Charlie...?

CHARLIE. *(Relenting.)* I'll see what I can do.

COBB. Is that coffee ready yet?

CHARLIE. You wanna cup?

COBB. I wanna bucket.

*(***CHARLIE** *pours coffee for* **COBB**.*)*

CHARLIE. What about him? Does he deserve a cup?

DANNY. I have a splitting headache. I'm chilled to the

bone. If you want me to be productive, I need caffeine.

COBB. Half-a-cup. Ya get the other half later.

> (**CHARLIE** *hands coffee to* **DANNY**, *then starts to exit.*)

Charlie, call down to maintenance again. Get an update on the forecast...it's hard to work in these conditions. *(Beat.)* And any word on our *special* guest?

CHARLIE. I'm sending a car to the airport.

> (**CHARLIE** *leaves.*)

COBB. Okay. Let's talk through these story notes. Consider our options.

DANNY. You should feel ashamed, Mr. Cobb. Looting my creative ideas.

COBB. You call these creative?

DANNY. They're *preliminary* notes.

COBB. Very preliminary. Barely *liminary*. Some of these I'm not sure are even notes. This one looks like a grocery list.

DANNY. Let me see that.

> *(He reads what is obviously a grocery list.)* Okay, I picked up a few things on the way to the airport.

COBB. And don't talk to me about shame. Shame is not an emotion producers are capable of feeling. Pride of accomplishment, maybe...acceptance of my glittering destiny, sure, those are things I'm able to feel...but shame is not among them.

> (**COBB** *fans out the papers on the coffee table.*)

And I wouldn't call this *looting*.

DANNY. What would you call it?

COBB. *Collating*. I'm arranging in order of merit. Assessing if there is *anything* here of *any* literary value.

DANNY. There's plenty, okay? You're sitting on a goldmine. I'm a bottomless pit of ideas.

COBB. Oh, right, right. *(He finds and reads one of* **DANNY**'*s* *ideas.)* "A man falls down a bottomless pit of ideas...and has to struggle with his overnight meteoric success as a playwright."

DANNY. That's still in its *germinal* phase.

CHARLIE. It's not an idea, it's a journal entry.

DANNY. There are ideas in there – I could pick up the phone and sell to a half-dozen Hollywood producers. Sight unseen!

COBB. Well, I believe that – 'cause if they actually *saw* 'em, they wouldn't give ya a nickel.

DANNY. You sayin' I don't know a good plot from a bad plot?

COBB. Who said anything about plot? I don't want plot – I want funny. If I detect the slightest hint of plot in the play you write me, I'll be very disappointed!

DANNY. *(Puffing himself up.)* You wanna know the difference between a good writer and a hack? A bad writer keeps what most writers throw out...a *good* writer throws out what most writers keep...but a *great* writer keeps what mediocre writers throw out, then panic and put back in.

COBB. That explains it: in a completely incomprehensible way.

DANNY. There's gotta be something in there that you respond to. On a gut level.

COBB. All right. *(He picks one out.)* How about this one? *(He reads another selection.)* "A stranger comes to town with a horrifying secret – "

DANNY. That's a classic set-up.

COBB. "He terrorizes the inhabitants of the small coastal village in which the story is set..."

DANNY. Act Two.

COBB. "...eventually betraying them all in despicable ways, until the townsfolk gather in the village square to commit *ritual suicide*...??"

DANNY. That's what we call in the trade, a "closed ending."

COBB. I think it's called a *terminal* diagnosis. "...they commit ritual suicide...while the mysterious stranger eats a picnic lunch with his family and watches the shocking proceedings unfold."

DANNY. It's an ironic coda.

COBB. Do I respond to this on a gut level? *Yeah* – it makes me wanna puke! *(Beat.)* This is one of your ideas? For a *comedy*??

DANNY. It's all about point of view.

COBB. *Whose* – whose point of you? The audience's? The slaughtered townsfolk? Or the *psychopath* who dreamt up the plot?

DANNY. It's a mood piece.

COBB. Yeah, I'm familiar with the mood: prevailing gloom...with a hint of doom!! How am I supposed to wring comedy from this?

DANNY. *(Quoting himself.)* "A great writer keeps what a mediocre..."

COBB. Yeah, yeah. *(Beat.)* What's the theme?

DANNY. Beware of strangers.

> *(**COBB** tears the sheet of paper in half.)*

COBB. Nobody will come to see this.

DANNY. I'd come to see it.

COBB. Nobody would *pay* to see it. And if I can't sell it on Broadway, what do I got? Bupkis!

DANNY. What do you think of the title? Can you at least use the title?

> *(He pieces the sheet of paper back together so he can read the title.)*

COBB. "Death Valley"? – Sure, the comic romp of the summer! You know what this is good for?

DANNY. Off-Broadway?

COBB. Fuel.

(He takes out a lighter and sets the notes ablaze, dropping them into a little silver trash can.)

DANNY. Okay, look Mr. Cobb – I'm gonna level with you. It hasn't been easy. After my Broadway debut my agent's phone was ringing off the hook. Offers galore! This one wanted a quiet character-driven drama. This one wanted me to adapt the great American novel. And this one wanted – as I'm sure *you* do – for me to simply repeat *exactly* the same thing I'd already achieved. The mechanical regurgitation of a classic comedy: broad enough to appeal to every theatergoer in the entire country; narrow enough to conform to the cultural zeitgeist; and slim enough to not tax the attention span. *(Brief pause.)* I just don't think it's possible, Mr. Cobb. I was lucky enough to have one popular hit. I just don't think lightning can strike twice in the same place.

COBB. Pass me that hair dryer.

*(**COBB** starts to walk off toward the bedroom with the hair dryer, but is stopped in his tracks by **DANNY**'s words.)*

DANNY. Why they liked it, I couldn't tell you. I don't think it was the best thing I ever wrote – nor is it the worst. It wasn't a literary home run. It was right down the middle, you know? A solid hit straight down the middle. The only thing that distinguished it from my half-dozen unknown plays that had come before, was... timing. The planets were aligned. We got the right director, thank Thespis. He cast the right actors. And we booked the right theatre. And for some *inexplicable* reason, the critics all came the same night, and hadn't had a bad day that day, and didn't feel in competition with this *unknown*, and...who knows why...they were not unkind. *(Pause.)* I hate to say it, Mr. Cobb, because I do have some faith in my own words. But I have a helluva lot *more* faith in my own words in the mouth of the right star saying 'em. *(Beat.)* Smartest thing I could do at this particular moment is take the money offered by MGM to make my play into a movie – let them screw it up if it's gonna get screwed up – just take the paycheck and run...and thank my lucky stars I got my fifteen minutes. Because I'm telling you: the pressure to repeat myself...it's just too much. A year ago I was on top of the world, now I'd settle for a cup of hot coffee and a pair of ears muffs. I had it all, Mr. Cobb... But I lost something, very recently, something more valuable to me than confidence.

COBB. What is that?

DANNY. Ah, doesn't matter. Sure, I'll write another play again someday...it might even be a good play...but how could anyone possibly judge it with any kind of objectivity without it being eclipsed by my first big hit? Which was – I have to admit – as much a surprise to me as it was to my agent, my producer, my family and my friends. There is such a thing as a fluke, Mr. Cobb...in life...and in art.

>（*Silence.*）

COBB. What horseshit!

>（*Beat.*）

That was a nice speech, Danny, but like most monologues in most plays – it was horseshit, didn't serve any real dramatic purpose, and basically just wasted time. Now, here's what's gonna happen.

>（**CHARLIE** *comes flying through the door with a Russian-style fur hat – a ushanka – which he tosses to* **DANNY.** **CHARLIE** *immediately pulls a large hotel envelope out from inside his jacket, pulls out an 8x10 of* **DANNY,** *and proceeds to sign it.*）

CHARLIE. Hope it fits.

DANNY. What's this?

CHARLIE. A *ushanka*! We got Russian tourists at the hotel.

COBB. *(In panic, looks through the peephole.)* Russians?

CHARLIE. They said thanks for the autograph.

(COBB is momentarily jarred but quickly regains his composure.)

DANNY. What autograph?

CHARLIE. *(Holds up the headshot he just signed.)* "I couldn't have done it without you: Nebraska Jones."

DANNY. How many of those have you forged?

CHARLIE. How many seats they got at the Majestic, Mr. Cobb?

COBB. Fifteen-hundred, give or take.

CHARLIE. We got enough for an eight-week run.

(DANNY dons the ushanka.)

DANNY. How do I look?

COBB. Like Chekhov.

CHARLIE. – On his deathbed in the Black Forest.

COBB. That doesn't help, Charlie.

(Crossing to CHARLIE.) What's the ETA?

CHARLIE. Any minute, sir.

DANNY. Oh, who's coming now? David Selznick?

COBB. Never you mind who – a secret weapon, that's who. Now...go get your typewriter. The clock is ticking!

(DANNY reluctantly exits to the bedroom.)

CHARLIE. Sir, you keep saying that: the clock is ticking.

COBB. Don't worry about it.

CHARLIE. Okay.

COBB. It's a convention.

CHARLIE. Okay.

COBB. In the theatre. To ratchet up the tension.

CHARLIE. The ticking clock.

COBB. Don't worry about it.

(DANNY reappears holding the typewriter case.)

And *you...* You're gonna start writing your new play –

DANNY. When?

COBB. Right now!

DANNY. For the record: I can't work on this thing.

>*(**CHARLIE** grabs the case from him, and sets up the typewriter on a small rolling table.)*

COBB. *(Threatening.)* Oh, yeah you will. You're not leaving Arizona until it's finished. Charlie and I are gonna read along as you generate pages. And no one sleeps until we've got a workable draft.

>*(**CHARLIE** rolls in a single sheet of paper, and wheels the table in front of **DANNY**.)*

Now type!

DANNY. I... I don't know where to begin.

COBB. How about the title?

DANNY. And you didn't care for *Death Valley?*

COBB. No, type!... *A Masterpiece of Comic Timing.*

DANNY. You gotta be kidding me.

COBB. Heat up the coffee, Chuck! Type!

>*(**DANNY** reluctantly begins to type the title page. Sitting there, wrapped in a blanket with the Russian hat on his head, he couldn't look more idiotic. We hear the hair dryer running as **CHARLIE** starts to reheat the coffee pot.)*

DANNY. Okay, Mr. Cobb, but no promises. I don't feel very funny right now.

CHARLIE. You look kinda funny.

DANNY. I can't guarantee this'll be a comedy.

COBB. You let me worry about that. If there's one thing I've learned in this business about comedy, it's...

>*(There is a knock at the door, then...)*

>*(The main door to the suite is thrown open, and in walks **NOLA HART**, dramatically.)*

NOLA. Ready for my audition, Mr. Cobb.

DANNY. Nola?

NOLA. You bastard!

    (Blackout.)

Intermission

ACT TWO

(Same suite. Night. Very late.)

*(AT RISE: **COBB** is sprawled out on the sofa fanning himself with a room service menu. He's in his boxer shorts and shirt sleeves, the cuffs rolled up, and his socks rolled down. Apparently, the A/C has not regulated itself, and they're again experiencing intolerable heat in the living room; however, as we shall discover in a moment, the bedroom is still perishingly cold.)*

*(At once through the door comes **CHARLIE** with a room service tray. He's changed into Bermuda shorts and a tank top. He immediately sets a bowl down in front of **COBB**.)*

CHARLIE. You order room service?

COBB. I didn't order soup.

CHARLIE. It's not soup.

COBB. I ordered baked Alaska.

CHARLIE. It was baked Alaska when I left the lobby.

> *(**COBB** dribbles some watery liquid off his spoon into the bowl, and pushes it aside.)*

COBB. Aaagh, just pour me a drink.

CHARLIE. The usual?

COBB. Double-usual.

> *(**CHARLIE** goes to the drinks table.)*

Did you get more ice?

CHARLIE. Yes, sir.

COBB. Good, 'cause I want ice, lots of ice.

(CHARLIE hands COBB a generous tumbler of bourbon, and then grabs the ice bucket.)

CHARLIE. Say when.

(He spoons several spoonsful of water into COBB's drink.)

COBB. That's not ice.

CHARLIE. It was when I left the lobby.

COBB. Alright! Just gimme that. *(He takes a big, welcome gulp of bourbon.)* I shouldn't have skipped dinner – it's the most important meal of the day. *(Beat.)* What time is it?

CHARLIE. Late. You don't wanna know.

COBB. How late?

CHARLIE. You know that meeting?

COBB. Uh-huh?

CHARLIE. The one you had today?

COBB. Uh-huh?

CHARLIE. All-day? Called "A Terrible Day"?

COBB. Yeah?

CHARLIE. It ain't over yet.

(COBB holds the glass of bourbon to his forehead to gain some relief from the heat.)

COBB. I think I'm coming down with something. Do I look pale?

CHARLIE. You have a naturally pallid complexion sir.

COBB. Is that good?

CHARLIE. In certain states. What are your symptoms?

COBB. They fluctuate. First, hot flashes…and then cold feet. Cold feet, and then hot flashes. It fluctuates rapidly between hot flashes and cold feet.

CHARLIE. I'm not a doctor, but you're either an Old Maid or a Bride-to-be.

COBB. This constant flux in temperature can't be good for the system. How's my pulse?

CHARLIE. *(Checking it.)* What pulse? Oh, *that* pulse. It's racing.

COBB. I'm under a lot of stress, Bascher. I've had a string of bad days in a row, I really need a break.

CHARLIE. What can I do, sir?

COBB. Just stick with me, to the bitter end. Will you do that?

CHARLIE. Of course.

COBB. You are a comfort to me, Charlie.

CHARLIE. That's a lovely sentiment. Thank you, sir.

COBB. I will deny ever having said it, of course, but it doesn't diminish the emotion.

> (**CHARLIE** *questions this, but says nothing.* **COBB** *crosses toward the bedroom door. Off, we can hear the faint clack-clack of typewriter keys in the other room.*)

So, how's it going in there? You checked on 'em lately?

CHARLIE. Every hour, on the hour. And I make a point of being emphatic.

COBB. I have to say: I think this emphatic thing has gone to your head.

CHARLIE. I like it there. It suits me.

COBB. You're becoming quite the little dictator.

CHARLIE. My mother would be proud. She always said I was too big for my britches. And now, for the first time in my life, I feel like I'm finally...filling my britches.

> (**COBB** *is not sure how to feel about this, but takes a step away from* **CHARLIE** *just in case he's speaking literally, not figuratively.*)

I'm finally getting the respect from people I deserve.

COBB. How do you know it's respect? Maybe it's intimidation.

CHARLIE. Aren't they the same thing?

COBB. Fair point.

CHARLIE. I owe it all to you, Mr. Cobb. You taught me

how to stand up for myself. How to get what I want in this grasping world, and not settle for second-best. You pointed out my boot straps, and explained what I was supposed to do with them. From here on out, I'm never gonna take "no" for an answer, and I *refuse* to get pushed around by anybody.

COBB. When you put it like that, you don't sound like the "model employee" no more.

CHARLIE. Mr. Cobb: I'll always be loyal to you.

(**COBB** *holds a finger to his mouth.*)

COBB. Sssshhh!

CHARLIE. What?

COBB. Listen: I don't hear typing.

CHARLIE. He's been somewhat resistant, Mr. Cobb.

COBB. In what way?

CHARLIE. To the idea of being forced to write a comedy, when he's so clearly in the mood for tragedy.

COBB. He's on commission: he'll write what I want him to write; and if it's not right, we'll rewrite it. Right?

CHARLIE. Right.

COBB. *Whattsamatter* with him? Is it that broad? Was it a bad idea bringing her out here? He doesn't seem to be happy to see her; if anything he's even gloomier.

CHARLIE. I caught him leafing through the wrong half of *The Agony and the Ecstasy* again.

COBB. *(Sighs.)* Did you confiscate it?

CHARLIE. I burned it in the sink. They could use a little warmth in there.

COBB. A/C still on full-blast in there, huh?

CHARLIE. It's like the Russian Front. Ice crystals have formed on their eyebrows.

COBB. Good. It'll keep 'em awake.

CHARLIE. And if they die, it'll keep 'em cryogenically stable.

COBB. What if...? Maybe we could open up the door

between the living room and the bedroom side? Even things out.

CHARLIE. I tried that earlier, sir.

COBB. And?

CHARLIE. We experienced a Chinook.

(The typewriter suddenly falls silent again, and we hear raised voices from the other room.)

COBB. Sssh-ssshh – ya hear that?

CHARLIE. Fighting?

COBB. *Not* typing! My ears are acutely attuned to the sound of people loafing on my dime!

CHARLIE. They've been engaged in heated discussion throughout the night.

COBB. I don't want discussion, I want dialogue. Funny dialogue.

CHARLIE. He's making headway, but he's still struggling with the plot.

COBB. We don't need plot. I told him that! *(Beat.)* You take a hundred jokes and put it in three acts, there's your plot.

CHARLIE. Whattaya do with the leftovers?

COBB. What leftovers?

CHARLIE. A hundred doesn't divide evenly in three.

COBB. Then you write an epilogue. *(Beat.)* Go check on 'em will ya? I want a status report. See how the narrative is shaping up.

CHARLIE. I'm on it, sir.

COBB. And if he refuses to type...

CHARLIE. Don't worry... I know what to do.

*(Before exiting into the bedroom, **CHARLIE** puts on a trench coat, and pulls up the collar. He experiences – and we hear – a blast of arctic air as he disappears into the bedroom.)*

(**COBB** *makes his way to the drinks table for another belt. As he does, the bedroom door opens again, and in strides* **NOLA HART**.)

(*She is wearing a full-length plush fur coat and Wellington boots. Again, we hear the blast of cold air, but the moment she's inside the living room area, she peels off the coat and tosses it onto the sofa, revealing that all she's wearing is a tropical top and colorful sarong underneath her winter garb.*)

NOLA. (*Luxuriating in the warmth.*) Oh, the weather's amazing out here. I should visit more often. Do you know there's color brochures in the bedroom describing the tropical climate in the living room?

COBB. You wanna drink?

NOLA. Please.

COBB. Whattaya drink?

NOLA. Virtually anything.

COBB. We got bourbon and more bourbon.

(*She spots the bowl of melted liquid on the coffee table.*)

NOLA. What's this?

COBB. Baked Alaska soup.

NOLA. I'll stick with bourbon.

(*He pours one.*)

COBB. You want ice?

NOLA. Just one cube.

(**COBB** *spoons in one spoonful of water into her glass.*)

COBB. Here ya go.

NOLA. Thanks, Mr. Cobb.

COBB. Call me Jerry.

NOLA. Thanks, Mr. Jerry.

(*They clink glasses and drink.*)

COBB. So.

NOLA. So.

COBB. Nola Hart.

NOLA. That's me.

COBB. And whaddayou got to say for yourself?

NOLA. Um… *Thanks* for bringing me all the way out here – what a surprise!

COBB. Look, I'm sorry I sprung this on ya.

NOLA. You sprung it all right! I haven't had a *spring* like that in years.

COBB. If I'd told you all the details, I don't think you'da come.

NOLA. I don't think I *would.*

COBB. Is it that bad? Take a look around. You're staying at one of the most luxurious hotels in the southwest.

NOLA. You know, you're right. I was standing in front of the bathroom mirror last night…that I had just scraped… when it started to sleet, then snow, then blizzard…it was sorta *magical,* you know? …But it made me think… this *can't* be the "dry heat" everyone talks about. *(Beat.)* How'd you find me?

COBB. Charlie. Mr. Bascher. He's resourceful.

NOLA. And very emphatic.

COBB. You noticed.

NOLA. He puts exclamation points on things you shouldn't put exclamation points on.

COBB. It's becoming tiresome.

NOLA. I find it…charming. And I like his little mustache. Makes him look like Clark Gable.

COBB. Sure, he looks like Gable, but he acts like Hitler.

NOLA. Well, I find him charming.

COBB. So did much of Europe!

NOLA. Oh, Mr. Cobb, where's your faith in humanity. You gotta trust people.

COBB. I got faith in humanity, just nobody I know personally.

>   *(He sits. Her glass is now empty.)*

NOLA. *(A thirsty Marilyn Monroe.)* What's a girl gotta do to get another drink around here?

COBB. *(Gulp!)* Ask like that.

>   *(He crosses to her.)*

Here, share mine. *(With great reverence.)* There is a long-standing tradition amongst my people...to share all sorts of...fluids with our honored female guests.

NOLA. Who's your people?

COBB. Men.

>   *(She stands and crosses away.)*

NOLA. Why'd you bring me here, Mr. Cobb? Was it for my talent, my brains, or my body? *(Beat.)* Or both?

COBB. Isn't it clear, Nola?

NOLA. No! No, my role in this little desert oasis fiasco of yours is entirely cryptic. I'm a classically trained actress, Mr. Cobb. I need to know my motivation.

COBB. Classically trained, huh?

>   *(She hands him a piece of rolled up paper.)*

NOLA. Here's my resume.

>   *(He starts to unroll it...and unroll it...and unroll it some more.)*

COBB. Impressive list of credits.

NOLA. I've studied Shakespeare, Kabuki and the Greeks. I've played all the great roles in Ibsen and Chekhov. And I'm intimately acquainted with the body of work of the great American dramatists – Miller, Williams, O'Neill. In fact... As my resume reflects, I've done intimate work *on* their bodies as well.

COBB. Wasn't Arthur Miller married to Marilyn Monroe?

NOLA. He was until he met me.

COBB. And wasn't Tennessee Williams...a homosexual?

NOLA. Well, he was until he met me.

COBB. But, come on, Nola... Eugene O'Neill is long dead.

NOLA. Are you sensing a pattern here? *(Beat.)* Okay, fella, you whisk me out here in secret. I barely get a word in edgewise before being cooped up in that *icebox* with *him*. I don't know what the story is – but no one seems the least bit interested *in me.* And I'm generally accustomed to everyone showing intense interest *in me.* If someone doesn't give me a through-line soon, I'm on the next flight back to California!

COBB. Okay, I'll level with ya, Nola. I need your help. With Danny. Is there any way you two could work things out?

NOLA. Are you asking me to prostitute myself for the sake of your project?

COBB. Not in those exact words.

NOLA. Well, what words would you use, exactly?

COBB. Can you *please* prostitute yourself for the sake of my project. *(Beat.)* Listen, listen!! I got everything riding on this script. I've invested a considerable amount of time and resources.

NOLA. I figured the conversation would swing that way.

COBB. What way?

NOLA. That's usually what it's all about, isn't it? Time? And resources?

COBB. This little venture...

NOLA. Oh, it's little now? A second ago it was *considerable.*

COBB. Look: Nola, I'm just saying...it would be easier-going if Danny wasn't so down in the dumps. So I would *appreciate* anything you can do to warm his spirits.

NOLA. Warm his spirits? Not in that room.

COBB. You know what I mean.

NOLA. Look, Mr. Cobb. I don't have anything to do with that man's disposition.

COBB. But you dumped him.

NOLA. He dumped me. And that's never happened before. Never.

Like *ever*.

Like...it's incomprehensible. I mean *look* at me!

COBB. But he said...

NOLA. I don't care what he said, Mr. Cobb. I haven't warmed his spirits in years. Danny Jones was morose long before I entered or left the picture. Writers are weird!

COBB. He told me that he recently experienced a loss like no other.

NOLA. Is that what he said?

COBB. To paraphrase.

NOLA. Well, he wasn't talking about me.

COBB. What was he talking about?

NOLA. You'd laugh if I told you.

COBB. Try me.

NOLA. No, I don't think I will. I think you'll just have to figure this one out yourself...to paraphrase.

COBB. Nola?

NOLA. Hey, you mind if I take off my boots? My ankles are swelling.

COBB. Be my guest.

(**NOLA** *slips her feet out of her boots.*)

NOLA. Aaaaahhh! That's so much better. I was getting trench foot in there.

COBB. *(Continuing on the same tack.)* Danny said he lost something more important to him than confidence – I assumed he was talking about you.

NOLA. No, but what a sweet thing to say.

COBB. And – pardon the indelicacy – I assumed you were only with him because of what he could do for your career.

NOLA. Listen here, Mr. Cobb – whatever success I've achieved is due entirely to my own industriousness. I don't owe anybody. I made it in this business the old-fashioned way.

COBB. Hard work and never giving up?

NOLA. Sleeping my way to the top. It's very time-consuming!

COBB. I admire your candor, Miss Hart. I don't know many women who could have a frank conversation of a highly sexual nature with a total stranger.

NOLA. You should get out more often.

Don't you like sexually aggressive women?

COBB. It reminds me of my childhood. As a teenager...

NOLA. Oh, god, I'm sorry, how insensitive of me. Did a relative abuse you?

COBB. No, as a teenager I liked sexually aggressive women and dreamed someday of meeting one.

> (**COBB** *is more than a little distracted by* **NOLA** *as she parades around before him.*)

NOLA. Yeah, well, I changed my ways. Experienced a reformation. I mean: sex and intimacy, intimacy and sex – it's all so distracting don't you think?

COBB. *(Distracted.)* I'm sorry, what?

NOLA. It took me a few years, but I can see now there's no profit in sleeping your way to the top.

COBB. You had a moral crisis?

NOLA. No, a bad back. My chiropractor told me if I kept it up at the rate I was going, I might reach the pinnacle of theatrical success, but I'd be in a wheelchair. So I made this solemn vow of chastity, a couple weeks back. It was a Saturday night. It was raining. I looked out the rain-streaked window and I said to myself, "Mary...you can never sleep with a man again, as long as you live."

COBB. You refer to yourself as "Mary"?

NOLA. *(Softly.)* Uh-huh.

COBB. I thought your name was Nola?

NOLA. I was in a play.

COBB. On stage?

NOLA. Yeah, last Saturday.

COBB. Mary's the character? In the play?

NOLA. Uh-huh.

COBB. And Mary made this vow of chastity?

NOLA. That's probably why I only made it to Wednesday, huh? I guess what I've learned is, you can never really change your nature.

COBB. Nola, you are quite the femme fatale.

NOLA. If that's a condition you get from sleeping around, I'm a prime candidate. But like I said, I've totally changed my ways. Tried to go cold turkey, in fact.

COBB. You considered celibacy?

NOLA. Yes, I considered it...seriously considered it...but the guy I was sleeping with at the time thought I should reconsider.

COBB. Boy, how selfish! Sounds like a typical actor.

NOLA. It was my chiropractor. No, sir, I've never made the mistake of sleeping with an actor. That was one of my iron-clad rules. I've only slept with agents, and publicists and directors and playwrights and...who am I leaving out?

COBB. Producers?

NOLA. I guess one or two of them as well.

COBB. At the same time?

NOLA. No, that was another one of my iron-clad rules. I feel funny saying this now, but in bed...in my experience...playwrights...have a lot of issues.

COBB. You mean their performance, their stamina?

NOLA. No, all the chit-chat. With Danny? Our pillow talk? Felt like a Noël Coward play. And foreplay...it was more like stage directions. *(She quotes* **DANNY** *in bed.)* "She enters seductively, approaching the bed in a sheer negligee."

COBB. Keep going.

NOLA. "First her hot lips on his neck, then lower... lower... please a little bit lower," – I mean I couldn't concentrate.

COBB. He said that? Out loud? When you were in bed? Making love?

NOLA. Sometimes he typed it up in advance so I could memorize it. *(Short pause.)* Writers are really weird! And always with the interruptions!

COBB. What interruptions?

NOLA. We'd be in the throes of wild abandon –

COBB. *(Mouthing the phrase silently.)* "Throes of wild abandon."

NOLA. – he'd think of a good line and have to reach over to the nightstand to scribble it down. You have any idea how frustrating it is to have your ecstasy punctuated by bouts of dramaturgy? Dramatis interruptus!

> *(The phone rings. COBB slowly turns to it in horror. He stands and crosses to answer it. We hear a muffled voice on the other end, vaguely threatening.)*

COBB. *(Into the phone.)* Nyet... Nyet...

> *(He hangs up and turns to NOLA, who has sprawled languorously on the couch.)*

...Nyet!

NOLA. I won't take Nyet for an answer.

COBB. *(An appeal.)* Nola please! I'm begging you!

NOLA. Okay, well now this feels like a normal conversation.

COBB. I have obligations. Y'unnerstand? To certain partners. Certain silent partners. Certain silent partners...who are Russian. *(Beat.)* And if those silent partners, don't see some progress on this project soon...they won't stay silent for long.

NOLA. Who are they...these silent partners?

COBB. Grotzky, Grotzky, Grotzky, Grotzky and Grotzky.

NOLA. Russian law firm?

COBB. Ukrainian quintuplets. Big, mean, psychotic Ukrainian quintuplets. *(Beat.)* So, Nola, please, tell me...help me...what's put Danny in this terrible funk?

(Pause.)

NOLA. All right, I'll tell ya –

(Beat.)

That man was once the love of my life, but now...

COBB. Yes?

NOLA. Well, *now...*

> *(The door to the bedroom opens, and a puff of snowflakes emits from the entryway.* **CHARLIE** *wheels in* **DANNY** *in a wheelchair. A piece of wood has been placed across the armrest, and the typewriter rests upon it.* **DANNY**'s *hands have been forcibly taped into position so that only his fingers are free to hit the keys.* **CHARLIE** *wheels* **DANNY** *to centre.)*

CHARLIE. Beep-beep, comin' through!

DANNY. *(Strenuously objecting.)* I strenuously object to this treatment.

CHARLIE. Okay.

DANNY. I'd like to lodge a formal complaint with the Dramatists Guild.

CHARLIE. You got it.

DANNY. I wanna talk to my agent!

CHARLIE. There's the phone, go right ahead.

> *(***DANNY** *tries in vain to reach out his hand to the phone.)*

DANNY. Aaaagh! Aaaaagggghhh!

COBB. Is that really necessary, Mein Fuhrer?

CHARLIE. I caught him red-handed, sir.

COBB. Doing what?

CHARLIE. *Not* doing what – he stopped writing.

DANNY. *(Like a revolutionary about to mount the scaffold.)* My mind is a blank!

CHARLIE. He was plotting his own death.

I found this in the typewriter.

> (**CHARLIE** *rips the current sheet of paper from the typewriter and hands it to* **COBB**.)

COBB. *(Eagerly.)* Let me see that – is it a good scene?

CHARLIE. It's a suicide note.

COBB. *(Pronouncing it like "cool.")* "Goodbye cuel world."

DANNY. "Cruel, *cruel.*"

CHARLIE. It's a typo.

DANNY. *(Pontificating.)* There is no reason to go on typing… there is no reason to go on living… *(Suddenly distracted.)* …wow, it's really warm out here. Someone take off my babushka.

> (**CHARLIE** *obliges him.*)

CHARLIE. Ushanka!

DANNY. *(Basking in the warmth.)* Oh that's nice. I read about this place in the brochures. I should have applied for a transfer sooner. *(Sees the bar. Perks up.)* Is that bourbon?

COBB. No bourbon for you. Not until I see some pages.

CHARLIE. What about you, Ms. Hart? Can I *get* you anything? Can I do you…anything?

NOLA. Well, aren't you a dear? Just keep being your adorably emphatic self.

> (**CHARLIE** *hands* **DANNY**'s *attaché to* **COBB**. *He takes out a couple dozen pages of typed manuscript and starts reviewing the material.*)
>
> (*The following exchange is like an exclusive, private conversation – like the characters forgot they were in a play.*)

DANNY. *(To* **NOLA**.*)* Hello, Nola.

NOLA. Danny.

DANNY. I see you moved to warmer climes.

NOLA. I needed to thaw out.

DANNY. I imagine that's tough with a heart made of ice!

> (**NOLA** *stands in protest.*)

NOLA. Look, Danny, you can insult me all you want.

DANNY. All right, siddown. This may take a while –

NOLA. I'm not gonna *stand* around while you disparage my character…

DANNY. I offered you a seat.

NOLA. …because we both know the reason why I left.

DANNY.	**CHARLIE.**
We do??	Why, why'd you leave?

NOLA. Don't act innocent.

DANNY. I was going for disinterested.

CHARLIE. Hey, show some respect for the lady. She came all the way from California to see you, pal.

NOLA. *(Impressed.)* Em-*phatic!*

> *(By now* **COBB** *has read through enough of the script to realize there's little of it that can be salvaged.)*

COBB. What is *this?*

DANNY. It's called a private conversation.

COBB. *(Re: the manuscript.)* This, *this!*

DANNY. The script.

COBB. This is the script?

DANNY. What I got so far, yeah.

NOLA. *(In spite of herself: kid, candy store.)* Is there a part for me?

DANNY. Perhaps.

NOLA. It better be juicy. I didn't give up a leading role in Sacramento for a piddly walk-on part in the second act in Scottsdale.

> **(COBB** *has to wrest the pages from* **NOLA***'s hands.)*

COBB. You feel confident you're heading in the right direction?

DANNY. Absolutely: the *only* direction.

COBB. Absolutely certain the subject lends itself to a comedic point of view?

DANNY. Certain. Absolutely. Gold mine. Of comedy.

COBB. You're not the least bit worried it might be construed, by some, to be somewhat *dark*...as comedies go?

DANNY. Not dark, it's light.

It's buoyant and hopeful.

COBB. And funny?

DANNY. I think so, yeah.

COBB. You're positive it lives up to its title?

NOLA. What's the title?

CHARLIE. *A Masterpiece of Comic Timing.*

NOLA. That's the title?

COBB/CHARLIE/DANNY. We've been over this.

NOLA. C'mon, let's hear it. Just the start. Just a teaser.

*(Everyone settles. **COBB** reluctantly turns to the first page of the manuscript and begins to read.)*

COBB. *(Clears his throat.)* "Act One, Scene One.

Russia, 1910. Curtain up: a dead body on stage.

Being torn apart by wolves."

Are you kidding me?

DANNY. Keep going, it picks up.

COBB. Picks up?

NOLA. I wanna hear, keep going.

CHARLIE. Mr. Cobb?

COBB. *(Reads.)* "The ravaged body belongs to a small boy name Alphonse, aged seven. Enter his mother, in tears." This is ridiculous, how can you construe this as funny?

DANNY. Give it a chance. I'm establishing a tone.

COBB. A tone? A tone?? We're three seconds in and you disemboweled a kid in front of his mother.

DANNY. Well, I...

COBB. What tone exactly did you wish to establish?

DANNY. Suspense can be an important element of comedy.

COBB. No it can't! Suspense is generally an important

element of *suspense!*

NOLA. Keep reading, I'm intrigued.

COBB. *(Oh, well then.)* She's intrigued!

NOLA. It's good, Danny. You haven't lost your touch.

DANNY. You haven't heard the mom's dialogue yet.

COBB. Oh, I can't wait.

NOLA. *(Jumping up.)* Here, let me read. *(A disclaimer.)* I usually don't do mothers. Unless it's pivotal. *(To* **DANNY.***)* Is it pivotal?

DANNY. Oh, yes.

NOLA. *(To* **COBB.***)* I'll read the mom, you do the kid.

COBB. The kid's *dead!* Devoured by wolves, remember?

DANNY. No, no, he has a line right before he expires.

COBB. "A line right before he expires –"?

DANNY. What?

COBB. A line right before he *expires...* *(To* **CHARLIE.***)* Did you hear what he just said? The kid has a deathbed confession.

DANNY. Not so much a confession as...an eternal truth.

COBB. I'm sure it's a zinger!

NOLA. *(Reprimanding* **COBB.***)* Come on, get in character.

COBB. I don't *wanna* be in character – I wanna be objective about this. Okay? I wanna let the words wash over me in a very objective way. I want to imagine I'm in the audience. On opening night. For the dazzling new comedy by Danny Nebraska Jones, and watch Mr. and Mrs. Liebowitz dissolve in a puddle of their own bitter tears when they watch little Alphonse being ripped apart *by wolves!!* ...G'head Charlie...

NOLA. Mr. Bascher? *(Handing the pages to* **CHARLIE.***)* Let us prepare.

> *(They head upstage to prepare for their entrance.)*

COBB. You g'head and read the kid. I'll be the Liebowitz's... figuring out how they can get their money back. Figuring out how they can shut us down for moral turpitude. G'head.

DANNY. *(In his own defense.)* This is realistic, Mr. Cobb. If you can't handle a little brutality in your comedy, then you're living in the wrong century.

COBB. Nobody wants to live in this century...the century of rabid wolves!

DANNY. Yes, they do!

COBB. Not theatre people! People who go to the theatre want to live in *another* century...that is far away from *this* one.

DANNY. What century?

COBB. A century in which love is possible?

DANNY. Love?

COBB. And hope prospers. And there's bright futures and *rainbows.*

DANNY. Seriously?

COBB. And people *learn* from toil and struggle – tough though it may be – and they aspire to a better life.

DANNY. That's in here. It's all in here if you'd give it a chance?

COBB. Where? When?

DANNY. Love and hope and a better life.

COBB. Is it coming up soon?? Because Alphonse has already lost a lot of blood.

DANNY. Be patient!!

COBB. Are there *any* rainbows?

DANNY. What? No!

COBB. Everybody likes a rainbow. Or just a ray of sunshine? Could you *squeeze in* a ray of sunshine between the pack of rabid wolves and the tearful entrance of the childless mother? A simple request.

DANNY. That doesn't make any sense! The play is set in Russia in 1910.

COBB. What, they don't got rainbows in Russia? You *research* that?

(**DANNY** *scoots his feet to advance on* **COBB**.)

DANNY. You're twisting my words.

COBB. I don't need to twist 'em, they're fairly twisted already.

DANNY. It's a historical piece.

COBB. That's not what I paid for!!

DANNY. I'm trying to take a cross-section of a particular culture, at a particular time and open it up, so it magnifies the lives of everyone, all of us, in the here and now. Where's your sense of history?

COBB. I got a sense of history. I got a sense it shouldn't go anywhere near my comedy!!

NOLA. (*To the entire room.*) Are we doing this or not?

> (**COBB** *puts some distance between himself and the scene unfolding.*)

COBB. Go ahead – I'll shut up.
I'll just be over here pulling my fingernails out. Or what Mr. Jones might call, "A light-hearted B-plot." G'head.

> (**NOLA** *heads for the door.*)

Where you goin'?

NOLA. I must exit, so that I may enter.

> (*She exits dramatically. Off, through the door we hear…*)

I am ready for my cue, Mr. Bascher.

CHARLIE. (*As Alphonse.*) "Momma, momma. Be careful, momma, the pack is still close at hand."

> (**COBB** *covers his face with a hand.*)

NOLA. (*As Momma.*) "Hush, Alphonse. Save your strength."

COBB. (*Can't help himself.*) Your strength?? For what??

DANNY. Ssssh! Have respect for the actors.

CHARLIE. "Momma, long ago…"

COBB. Please don't tell me his deathbed confession is in the form of a *monologue*. You're *really* gonna stretch this out – lights up: a kid bleeding out centre stage: and now we've gotta suffer through his *monologue?*

DANNY. There's *no* monologue. It's the mom who speaks now.

COBB. Thank heaven for small mercies.

> (**NOLA** *launches in.*)

NOLA. "Your death shall not be in vain."

> (**COBB** *raises his hand.*)

COBB. Can I make a comment?

DANNY. If you must.

COBB. It's an interesting line. The mother's line.

DANNY. Thank you.

COBB. "Your death shall not be in vain." Did I get that right?

> (**DANNY** *nods.*)

Interesting.

I just have a *feeling…*

DANNY. Uh-huh.

COBB. It might be more *effective…*

DANNY. Yes?

COBB. If the line occurred at the *end* of a powerful epic struggle, you know? During *which* we'd *actually* gotten to know who the hell Alphonse is…rather than at the *start* of a broad comedy in which we don't know Alphonse from a hole in the head – or in this case, a hole in the *bowel.*

NOLA. *(A serious suggestion.)* I don't know, I think the right actress could sell it.

COBB. *Sell* it? The right actress could *sell* this moment? I don't think you could give this moment away *for free*!!

DANNY. You know, if you're gonna nit-pick every single line…

COBB. Danny, I need the dialogue to be punchy.

DANNY. Punchy?

COBB. I need it to be playful and punchy. Light and playful and punchy.

DANNY. You don't think it's punchy?

COBB. No.

DANNY. If this isn't punchy dialogue, Mr. Cobb, I don't know what it is.

COBB. Bludgeony!
　Kid, it needs to be light as a feather.
　Imagine a shuttlecock.
　A game of badminton.
　Not force, finesse!
　Light banter, back and forth, back and forth.
　Poff-poff, poff-poff!

DANNY. I think I wrote banter.

COBB. No, Danny, no.

DANNY. How do you know where it's going? You don't know where it's going.

COBB. Yes I do.

DANNY. You only read four lines.

COBB. But I see the direction you're heading.

DANNY. And what direction is that?

COBB. Nowhere fast!! I want witty repartee amongst the glitterati of high society.

DANNY. And how'd you characterize this?

COBB. The transcript of the Nuremburg Trials.

DANNY. You know, the critic from *The New York Times* said my dialogue was groundbreaking.

COBB. In this case I'd have to agree!
　It'll break the ground, dig a shallow grave and bury the entire production.

NOLA. Mr. Cobb, can I interrupt...?

COBB. Ordinarily, yes, but this time, no! Stop! Stop!! This is nuts. This ain't comedy. I'm not even sure this is *tragedy*. It's beyond...

DANNY. Realism dictates...

COBB. "Realism," "pacifism," "nihilism," there is no "*ism*" to describe what you did here, kid. *Botulism?* Maybe that comes close.

CHARLIE. *(Stepping in with authority.)* We just need to rewrite the start. Change a couple variables. A slight comic recalibration.

COBB. That's right. Charlie's right. Some of it may be salvageable.

DANNY. Salvageable? You realize I'm sitting here, right? Taped to a wheelchair. Forced against my will to write something to order, something I feel is trite and soulless. Just because I cashed your check?

COBB. You cashed six of them.

DANNY. Cashed six of your checks. I can't be bought, Mr. Cobb!!

COBB. Did it occur to you to read the fine print of our contract? Which clearly states: "THIS CONTRACT MEANS YOU BEEN BOUGHT AND PAID FOR, YOU SONOFABITCH!!"

> *(**CHARLIE** senses impending danger and pushes **COBB** off through the bedroom door, then returns to the drinks table. **NOLA** has been reading ahead in the script, and is not happy.)*

NOLA. Danny, I have a bone to pick with you. I don't have a very big part in this play. You said the mother was pivotal.

DANNY. She is.

NOLA. *(Referring to the script.)* She dies in the first act.

DANNY. A death *is* pivotal!

NOLA. *(Waving the pages in the air.)* Not if it happens on page three!!

> *(**COBB**, now calmer, reappears through the bedroom door. He takes a deep breath, tries to regain composure.)*

COBB. I'm sorry. It's the heat. And the lack of something in my glass.

(CHARLIE quickly hands COBB a drink.)

COBB. *(Cont.)* Now. We're here to help. Make sure you're on the right track before we send you back to Siberia. Charlie, *paper!*

> *(CHARLIE puts another sheet of paper in the typewriter.)*

Okay, I talk, you type.

DANNY. For the record: this is a form of abuse.

COBB. I would have to agree. I couldn't listen to another word. *(Points to the typewriter.)* Now type.

DANNY. And what if I refuse?

> *(Silence. Everyone looks at DANNY, and then at COBB.)*

COBB. Adolf?

> *(And this is the moment CHARLIE's been waiting for – he is both emphatic and surprisingly intimidating. At the bar he slowly slices a wedge of lime with a knife in a sinister fashion.)*

CHARLIE. There's a reason we left your fingers free.

DANNY. *(Unsure he wants the answer.)* Why…?

CHARLIE. So they'd be easier to cut off if you refused to type.

COBB. *(Sotto voce; didn't know he'd go that far.)* Jesus Christ!

DANNY. *(Indignant.)* Are you…*threatening* me?

COBB. No, he's raising the stakes, you schmuck! We're giving you a free *writing* lesson! You think this opening scene of yours with the bloodshed is funny, but severed fingers…not so funny? Where's your sense of humor, Danny?

DANNY. I'm duct-taped to a wheelchair and a typewriter!! It's creative enslavement.

COBB. No it's not.

DANNY. It's indentured servitude.

COBB. No it's not.

DANNY. Then what would you call it?

COBB. Show business.

>   *(Beat.)*

You gotta trust us, Danny. I'm tellin' you...no matter how you spin it...the dead kid scene won't fly. Because what you got...? ...*All* you got is a dead kid. Comedy evolves, tragedy devolves. It's tough to climb aboard the merriment express from a disembowelment. From the point of view of general *mirth*, disembowelment doesn't get you out of the station.

DANNY. Then what do *you* suggest?

COBB. What do I suggest? I'm just the producer. I'm just the guy assuming all the risk. I'm just the guy putting all the money on the line hoping Mr. and Mrs. Liebowitz don't file an *injunction* before the intermission – *if* they last that long. Let us help you, Danny, at least *try* to get them to the intermission. Not even the end – the intermission. Hell, by the end, I'll be in the bar next door with all the other characters you wanna kill in the first act of your comedy who decide not to stick around for the curtain call!!

NOLA. I have never missed a curtain call in my life! Even plays I wasn't *in*.

COBB. At least let's engineer, together, a solid opening, huh? Even if we run out of steam toward the end.

DANNY. Fine.

NOLA. I'm in.

CHARLIE. Me too, boss.

NOLA. As long as I still get my death scene.

COBB. Here's a suggestion:

DANNY. Yeah?

COBB. And I think it honors the original intent.

DANNY. Okay.

COBB. Act One, Scene One."

DANNY. I'm listening.

COBB. "Russia, 1910. Curtain up: a dead '*something*' on stage."

DANNY. A dead what?

CHARLIE. Anything but a kid.

COBB. Anything *other* than a kid.

We'll figure it out later.

DANNY. Dog.

COBB. No.

CHARLIE. *(Isn't it obvious?)* Man's best friend.

NOLA. Frog?

COBB. Better. Don't feel you have to be limited. There are lots of things, as an audience, we would like to see dead...

NOLA. There is?

COBB. And might even laugh at.

DANNY. Can you give me an example?

COBB. Charlie, give him an example?

CHARLIE. Anyone from the IRS.

DANNY. Really?

COBB. Because no one actually *knows* anyone who works for the IRS. Do you? Do you? No.

DANNY. But what if there's someone in the audience who works for the IRS.

COBB. That'll never happen.

DANNY. Or someone who's married to someone who works for the IRS.

COBB. No one would have them.

DANNY. Or even just someone who knows a friend-of-a-friend-of-a-friend who's casually acquainted with someone who works for the IRS.

COBB. Such improbabilities are not my concern.

Trust me, people who work for the IRS don't go to the theatre.

DANNY. Why not?

COBB. They're too busy auditing the people who go to the theatre and claim it as a business expense. *(Beat.)*

Litmus test: what's funnier? Dead kid named Alphonse aged seven? Dead guy in polyester suit who works for the IRS?

DANNY. *(Relents.)* IRS guy, I guess.

COBB. See? We've all learned something today. What else? Other suggestions for the dead kid rewrite?

NOLA. Parakeet.

COBB. Good. Yes. A dead parakeet.

CHARLIE. *(To **NOLA**.)* You're good at this!

NOLA. *(Quickly, under breath.)* Classical training.

DANNY. Why's that funny I don't know why it's funny?

COBB. Charlie, tell him why it's funny.

CHARLIE. Because it has a "k" in it.

COBB. "Parakeet" has the letter "k" in it.

DANNY. The letter "k"?

COBB. All words with the letter "k" are funny. You don't know this? Have you spent any time at all contemplating the nature of humor? The rule of three, the rule of k, the rule of...

DANNY. What...?

COBB. Leaving things out.

DANNY. Is any of this true? Is the k-thing true?

CHARLIE. Test the theory.

> *(Brief pause.)*

DANNY. "Pickle."

> *(**CHARLIE** and **NOLA** laugh.)*

COBB. That's funny.

DANNY. "Pork barrel spending."

> *(**NOLA** and **CHARLIE** laugh.)*

COBB. Yep, phrases too...very funny. Nola? Wanna give it a try? *Cities.* Cities that include the letter "k." Pick a city, any city.

NOLA. Poughkeepsie. Hackensack.

COBB. Funny.

NOLA. Detroit.

COBB. Not so funny.

  States:

CHARLIE. North Dakota, South Dakota.

COBB. Good one. This is tricky. Which is funnier?

NOLA. North?

COBB. Do you know why?

> (**DANNY** *shakes his head.*)

  Me neither.

CHARLIE. Closer to Canada.

COBB. Yep, that could be why.

  Nola. Go international, expand your horizons.

NOLA. Marseilles? Geneva?

> (**COBB** *shakes his head.*)

COBB. Not funny.

NOLA. Timbuktu.

  Gdansk.

COBB. Funny! It's a never-ending fount of funny.
  The "k."

  It even applies to volcanoes.

DANNY. There's nothing funny about volcanoes.

COBB. That's what you'd think.

  But you tell me: "Two volcanoes walk into a bar."
  Which is funnier – Mt. Vesuvius? Or Krakatoa?

NOLA & CHARLIE. Krakatoa.

COBB. Krakatoa hands down!

> (**CHARLIE** *starts to wheel* **DANNY** *around the
> room, and toward the bedroom, in the wheelchair.*)

CHARLIE. Sports, Danny, you like sports?

DANNY. I guess.

CHARLIE. Why, what do you do with a basketball?

DANNY. Bounce it?

CHARLIE. Try again.

DANNY. Throw it?

CHARLIE. Again.

DANNY. Stuff it?

CHARLIE. *Warmer.*

DANNY. Dunk it!

CHARLIE. *There* ya go!
And if you're not *bouncing* a basketball, you're...?

DANNY. Dribbling?

COBB. B's are good also.

CHARLIE. A "b" is as good as a "k" to a blind horse

DANNY. That doesn't make any sense.

COBB. Doesn't have to. Now go write!

DANNY. How am I gonna work things with the letter "b" and "k" into the plot without it sounding totally contrived?

COBB. Haven't you been listening? Forget plot. Forget it. Forget you ever heard that offensive word "plot." Plot is the death of funny. It's like a sauce.

DANNY. Sauce?

COBB. A reduction sauce. The more you reduce the plot the more intense and satisfying the flavor of the jokes.

DANNY. You can't possibly believe that.

COBB. You want depth? You want character? Write tragedy. In tragedy you don't need to be funny, and you can have all the plot you want. G'head, layer on the plot. Thick as you please!

DANNY. That's the stupidest thing I ever heard.

COBB. It also has the added advantage of being true.

DANNY. It's a sweeping generalization.

COBB. Professor Charlie, tell him.

CHARLIE. Greatest play ever written?

DANNY. Err, I don't know.

NOLA. *Medea.*

COBB. *Wrong!*

NOLA. *(Citing her own resume.)* Which I played in 1954.

DANNY. *Hamlet?*

CHARLIE. All right, *Hamlet.* Is it funny?

DANNY. There are some jokes in there, yeah.

COBB. How many? Count them. Do you know how many?

DANNY. Not off the top of my head.

COBB. There aren't many, trust me. And the best ones happen after he's dead!

DANNY. Why would I count the jokes?

COBB. Audience does. They count 'em.

DANNY. No they don't.

COBB. In comedy they do.

DANNY. Why not in drama?

COBB. There's nothing to count. Except corpses. At the end they go, "Everyone's dead, it musta been good." At the end of comedy they go, "Nobody laughed, it musta been bad." It's called the math of mirth. *(Beat.)* It's a scientific fact.

CHARLIE. *Hamlet?* How many corpses?

DANNY. *(Starts to do the math with his fingers.)* Err…

COBB. Come on, it'll be on the midterm.

CHARLIE. Nine. Count 'em. Nine.

DANNY. But that's not plot.

COBB. Sure it is. What's the definition of plot?

NOLA. Stuff that happens.

COBB. What happens in *Hamlet?* Corpses happen. Left and right. It's nothing but corpses. "Hey, look a corpse!" "What do you think happened?" Hamlet happened, that's what!

CHARLIE. The King, The Girlfriend, the nosey Girlfriend's Dad, The Queen, The Other King, The Frat Boy/slash nosey Girlfriend's Brother, The Guys who were hired to kill The Guy, and then The Guy Himself: the Prince of Denmark. Nine.

COBB. The bodies pile up faster than the jokes. So…as a

working theory... I'm gonna suggest we try to remove as many corpses from your play as possible.

CHARLIE. And we try to...

DANNY. Reduce the plot...

COBB. In order to...

DANNY. Intensify the humor.

COBB. Atta boy!

So...to get back to the original question. Can we come up with anything funnier in the opening scene, than a dead kid?

DANNY. Okay, okay. Um.

(He thinks about anything that might be funnier than a dead kid.)

COBB. You got lots to choose from. Take your time.

DANNY. A dead bouquet of flowers.

NOLA. Flowers?

COBB. While flowers are not exactly *funny*, it's a marked improvement over the dead kid.

DANNY. A dead puppet?

COBB. Puppets aren't alive and I'm not doing a fucking puppet show! They freak me out, I hate 'em.

DANNY. Okay. A dead raccoon.

NOLA. Awww, they're cute.

CHARLIE. Skunk. A dead skunk. Nobody likes skunks.

NOLA. Plus it has a "k."

DANNY. Raccoon has a "k."

COBB. It has a thing that *sounds* like a "k" but technically no "k," therefore not funny. Skunks: I think we got it.

DANNY. "Nobody likes skunks"? Another sweeping generalization.

COBB. Well, if you gonna generalize, might as well be a sweeping one!

DANNY. Some people like skunks.

COBB. Which people?

DANNY. Some people.

COBB. Do these people go to the theatre?

DANNY. How would I know that?

COBB. I'll tell you how, *here's* how. You got two plays: one opens with a dead kid torn apart by wolves? One opens with a dead skunk. *(Beat.)* My money's on the skunk-play being funnier!

DANNY. But, but: some people love animals. "All creatures great and small," even a flea...

COBB. Yeah, but those people shouldn't go to the theatre.

DANNY. Why?

COBB. Because they got no sense of humor!! They should stay home and save fleas if that's their thing. I'm just trying to make a point here, Danny, about the scale of death one can get away with in a comedy versus a tragedy. That's all. Consider the container.

CHARLIE. Let's move on.

DANNY. What about the wolves?

COBB. What about the wolves?

DANNY. Are you comfortable with wolves disemboweling the...what is it now...the skunk?

COBB. Let's go with a skunk. We can change it in previews.

> (**DANNY** *types a few lines. Something about skunks.*)

NOLA. *(Raising her hand.)* Can I ask a question about my character?

COBB. *(Before she's even finished asking the question.)* No.

DANNY. Okay, so...now what are we thinking?

COBB. Vis-à-vis the wolves?

CHARLIE. I'm thinking: does it have to be a pack of wolves? What else could it be if not wolves?

> *(They all think.)*

DANNY. Communists? *(They all look at him.)* I don't know. It fits.

COBB. But is it funny? The litmus test, that's *always* the litmus test…is it funny? Let's think about this.

(They all think about it.)

Commies or wolves?

Wolves or commies?

Anyone?

CHARLIE. Sir, I think we achieved the impossible. We came up with two things that are equally *unfunny.*

NOLA. Let's not worry about this now.

COBB. *(In agreement.)* Read me back the opening with the changes.

DANNY. "Act One, Scene One. Russia, 1910. Curtain up: on a dead…skunk. Being torn apart by 'something funny we'll decide at a later date.'"

*(**NOLA** is preparing for her entrance.)*

COBB. *(To **NOLA**.)* Okay, now enter the mother.

*(**NOLA** starts to muster tears.)*

What are you doing?

NOLA. What is says in the script: entering "in tears."

COBB. That's not what it says.

(Shows him the page.)

NOLA. It says it right here.

COBB. It just says "tears." Doesn't depict the nature of the tears. Do they have to be tears of despair?

NOLA. What else would they be?

COBB. Joy?

NOLA. Her son just died.

COBB. No he didn't. Try to keep up. There is no dead kid no more. Just a skunk, that's all…nothing to get broken up about. Okay, now see what I did there? I turned the thing on its head. Always been turning the thing on its head. Why?

DANNY. Because it's funnier?

COBB. Because it's funnier.

NOLA. But, but…

COBB. The tears…don't have to be tears of despair. They could be tears of joy. Couldn't they? Couldn't they?

DANNY. Because she witnessed the death of a skunk?

NOLA. A *pet* skunk she named Alphonse?

COBB. Look: maybe my direction is not clear. Comedy is about context – can we all agree on that?

> *(They all agree on that.)*

I'm just asking you to *push* the text, *challenge* the material and, and –

DANNY. Turn it on its head?

COBB. Thank you! Look at the problem the other way around. What does the mom say? Nola –

NOLA. "Hush, Alphonse, save your strength. Your death shall not be in vain." Which doesn't track now. Danny, I think my character is profoundly…what's the word…?

DANNY. Complex?

NOLA. Badly written!

COBB. Are you saying you can't play it?

NOLA. I can play anything, Mr. Cobb. I've been known to coax the most flaccid material to life.

COBB. I don't doubt that.

DANNY. Flaccid??

NOLA. But I'm sorry, Danny… I'm beginning to think this material is beneath me.

DANNY. *That's* ironic…for someone who's spent the majority of their acting career in that exact position!!

CHARLIE. *(Coming to NOLA's defense.)* You're starting to get on my nerves, there, bub!

DANNY. You don't scare me, little man.

COBB. Focus, Charlie, it's your line. As the skunk.

CHARLIE. "Momma, momma, be careful. The pack is still close at hand."

NOLA. Is it still a pack of wolves? Or a pack of "something funny TBD"? I'm not sure this version is any funnier – I just think now it's totally cryptic.

DANNY. The material is not beneath you Nola – it's *beyond* you!

Too high-brow!

Too multi-layered.

Too...

NOLA. There is no part beyond my range! I'm a chameleon, Mr. Cobb.

COBB. Oh, yeah?

NOLA. Every time I step foot onstage, I'm a different person!!

DANNY. Sometimes in the same play!! Now stop kvetching and say the damn lines!!

NOLA. Can someone please tell me my motivation??

COBB. Your paycheck!!

NOLA. *(Suddenly falling in line.)* Well, why dincha say that?

COBB. *(Sounding academic.)* I don't wanna sound too academic, but... You're getting hung up on "meaning." Comedy doesn't necessarily have to "mean" anything.

NOLA. *(Skeptical.)* It doesn't?

COBB. No. In fact!! ...I would posit that comedy is enhanced by its general *lack* of meaning. Take...take for example the "whoopee" cushion.

DANNY. A wha...a whoopee cushion?

COBB. What does it do?

NOLA. It...

COBB. G'head.

DANNY. It farts?

COBB. It farts. The "whoopee" cushion makes a noise which sounds very much like a human gaseous eruption and is therefore funny. But it doesn't *mean* anything. It has no context.

NOLA. Sure it does.

COBB. What does it mean?

NOLA. That a person farted.

COBB. But only in the *abstract*!

NOLA. No, in the *practical*. It sounds *so much* like an actual fart that it's funny, because it might have theoretically been an actual fart, but actually it's so much *better* than an actual fart, because it has all of the benefits and none of the responsibility.

COBB. *(To* **CHARLIE.***)* Why did we fly her out here again?

DANNY. How can one fart in the abstract?

COBB. If you keep raising these larger philosophical questions we might as well quit writing a comedy. You're getting off topic.

CHARLIE. No, I'd like to know the answer to that, actually.

> *(Silence. Everyone ruminates on this like it's the big riddle of the universe.)*

COBB. Okay, the meaning is being muddied. Look, look... the revision process is a delicate one. Yeah? I don't expect us to get everything right first time out... but if we, you know, *line-by-line,* nudge it in the right direction... I feel we'll have made tremendous strides today...and this day might *actually* not be as bad as I imagined it. So...it doesn't all track. You fix one thing in a script, you break something else...one step forward, three steps back...that's the creative process. And sometimes you just gotta throw it all out the window.

CHARLIE. *(By the window.)* It'll have to be *this* window, because the one in the bedroom is still frozen shut.

COBB. *(He's losing his cool.)* The basic set-up: a dead skunk...

DANNY. A dying skunk...

COBB. There's a skunk in the process of expiring onstage...

NOLA. In walks the mother...

DANNY. Doesn't have to be a mother now...

COBB. In walks a woman.

NOLA. Who is she?

COBB. It's a mystery – now get off stage!

(He shoves **NOLA** *out the front door. She turns and is about to protest, when –* **COBB** *slams the door in her face.)*

DANNY. She could be anybody. She could be...any woman...*every* woman. *(To audience.)* Someone out there in that great big universe.

*(***NOLA** *re-enters, grandly, like Eleonora Duse.)*

NOLA. "Hush, Alphonse, save your strength. Your death shall not be in vain."

CHARLIE. Who's she talking to?

COBB. It's a big fuckin' mystery!

DANNY. She breaks the fourth wall. "Your death shall not be in vain."

*(***NOLA** *takes her cue, walks downstage, and breaks the fourth wall.)*

NOLA. "Your death shall not be in vain."

DANNY. *(An epiphany.)* She's talking to us. She's reaching out. Desperate to make a connection.

CHARLIE. *Then* the whoopee cushion!

COBB. YOU KNOW WHAT, FORGET IT...maybe this isn't a comedy after all! It's an absurdist piece. They're *oddly* becoming quite fashionable these days, god knows *why*...but why swim against the tide? The world is divided into two kinds of people – those who see things through a comic lens, and those who prefer to shove that lens up their short-sighted asses. I know that didn't make sense – but it's getting late! And I'm running out of time.

(There is an ominous banging at the door. Everyone jumps. Instinctively, **CHARLIE** *heads for the door.)*

Don't answer it!

DANNY. *(Shouting out, an epiphany.)* I got it, I got it!! I know what to do. I know what to do, Mr. Cobb. I know how to fix it.

COBB. You do? How?

DANNY. I'm gonna burn it!!

NOLA. What?

DANNY. Give me the pages, all of them, give me all the pages.

> *(They all hand back the pages from the manuscript.)*

Gimme your lighter, Mr. Cobb.

> *(**COBB** takes out his lighter.)*

COBB. You sure kid, I thought some of this stuff, the stuff with the parakeet had potential.

DANNY. I think the bravest act of creativity I can perform today is to destroy what I've already written...

> *(**COBB** hands his lighter to **DANNY**.)*

...and from those *ashes* will rise again...a funnier play...a play devoid of wolves and parakeets, dead children, communists or grieving mothers...and will include... some other things which might actually be *genuinely* funny. Like, like...some *references*...like, for example...

CHARLIE. Uh-huh?

DANNY. Well I can't think of anything off the top of my head...but, I've learned enough to trust the process. And to, I don't know...

COBB. Do things in threes?

DANNY. Do things in threes...

NOLA. Wait, what are we doing in threes?

DANNY. And that timing...

COBB. Uh-huh.

CHARLIE. Timing...?

DANNY. Timing is in many ways...

NOLA. What?

DANNY. More important...than...plot!

> *(There is a second loud pounding at the door. Everyone jumps again. **CHARLIE** once again heads for the front door.)*

COBB. I *said*, don't answer it! Danny, quick, burn it...burn all this Russian shit and start again.

DANNY. Oh, boy... I'm not sure I can do it anymore.

COBB. Sure you can, kid.

DANNY. No, I mean... I can't *(Struggling with the lighter.)* ... light the damn thing!! *(Beat.)* Oh, who am I kidding... even if I did have the guts to burn it, I just don't think I have the confidence to start again.

CHARLIE. What are you talking about?

DANNY. Ever since I lost the most important thing in my life...ever since she went away...

COBB. *(To NOLA.)* I'm tellin' ya, he's talking about you.

NOLA. No he's not.

DANNY. I've felt so empty and bereft.

CHARLIE. Who's he talking about?

DANNY. *(Wistfully.)* Olivetti...oh, Olivetti! *(Tragically.)* Please come back to me...!!

NOLA. *(Rolling her eyes.)* Oh, brother!

CHARLIE. Who the hell is Olivetti?

COBB. The other dame. It's gotta be.

NOLA. No it's not.

(**CHARLIE** *suddenly snaps.*)

CHARLIE. Okay, look, pal – I've had just about enough outta you!! I don't think my boss here can stand another bad day. His cardiologist called this morning to schedule his annual coronary. For the third time this week! When I took this job I swore an oath I'd deliver ONE GODDAMNED GOOD DAY ON MY WATCH!! And I've decided *it's today*! Today is the day!!

NOLA. There he goes again with the exclamation points!

CHARLIE. You are gonna *deliver* this script...come hell or high water...and frankly, I don't care if I have to write it *myself*.

DANNY. Ever hear of copyright??

CHARLIE. I would, however, for legal reasons, prefer it be done on *your* typewriter, with *your* literary *fingerprints*

ALL OVER IT!!

> (**CHARLIE** *grabs the knife from the bar and approaches* **DANNY**.)

DANNY. Help!! Help!!

COBB. Charlie, Charlie.

NOLA. *(Is she turned on by* **CHARLIE***?)* My God!

CHARLIE. C'MERE YOU SONOFABITCH!

COBB. I've created a monster.

CHARLIE. C'mere you *hack*! Thumbs first, then the pinkies!

COBB. *(In the commotion.)* It's okay kiddo. Put down the knife.

> (**DANNY** *struggles to get away by scooting the wheelchair backwards as fast as he can.* **CHARLIE** *is about to sever one of* **DANNY**'s *fingers, when he suddenly clutches his chest.)*

Charlie?

NOLA. Charlie?

DANNY. What, what??

COBB. He don't look so good.

CHARLIE. *(Through gritted teeth.)* I really didn't see that coming!

> (**CHARLIE** *collapses.*)

COBB. *(More surprised than concerned.)* He looks like I imagined *I'd* look when I finally had my heart attack.

> (**NOLA** *straddles* **CHARLIE**.)

NOLA. *(Slapping his face to revive him.)* Stay with me, Charlie!! Stay with me.

> (**CHARLIE** *is groaning with each slap.*)

Everyone, stay clear. I need to perform mouth-to-mouth resuscitation.

DANNY. Oh, stop being so obvious – if ya like the guy just fess up.

NOLA. A man's life is at stake, Danny. Can you stop being so self-involved for just one second? *(Beat.)* How's my hair?

(**NOLA** *begins to perform CPR. Everyone is mesmerized. It looks less like "critical care" and more "throes of passion." After a moment,* **CHARLIE** *finally splutters back to life, smiling intensely, breathing heavily, delirious.*)

COBB. Hey, kid, welcome back. You gave us quite a scare. Don't upstage me like that again, okay?

CHARLIE. Wha' happen?

NOLA. *(Breathless.)* Well, your heart stopped beating. Your life was slowly ebbing away. Brain activity went down to zero. And you were teetering on the brink of death.

CHARLIE. When you say it like that, it sounds like a bad thing.

(**NOLA** *takes the knife from* **CHARLIE** *and approaches* **DANNY** *slowly – she finally releases him from his bonds.*)

NOLA. Danny, I must be cruel to be kind. I know you're troubled, I know you're in pain. But it's writer's block, get over it!! Sometimes life requires us to set aside our petty problems and rise above 'em. Mr. Cobb placed his total faith in you.

(**COBB** *looks awkwardly away.*)

Which is something I could never do, not fully. Because there was always one thing that stood between you and me and happiness.

DANNY. What?

NOLA. Your typewriter. *(Beat.)* Jerry had faith from the get-go. So did Charlie. I envy their singular focus, to pool their energies and considerable funds...to invest in your talent. To believe in you. It was something I could never do. And I'm sorry, Danny. I'm so very sorry. Now, I'm off back to Sacramento, where I'll be playing a brilliant but troubled nineteen-year-old ingénue who discovers the cure for several deadly diseases while defending Europe from Hitler's Hordes in the French

Resistance – a sufficiently complex and age-appropriate role for me.

> *(She starts for the door.)*

DANNY. This is not my typewriter.

COBB. What?

DANNY. *(To* **COBB.***)* Mr. Bascher *whisked* me so fast from the airport, I didn't notice he'd picked up the wrong typewriter case until I got to the hotel. *(Beat.)* You have *any idea* how sentimental we writers are about our tools of the trade? Why do you think I've been in such a foul mood the last twenty-four hours?

COBB. That was the cause of your melancholy?

DANNY. No, I was faking that.

CHARLIE. I knew it.

DANNY. Melancholy has no cause. I just enjoyed idling away the hours with... General Malaise.

> *(***COBB*** and ***CHARLIE*** laugh.)*

NOLA. *(To* **COBB.***)* Told you you'd laugh.

COBB. But Danny why didn't you tell us sooner? Why wait 'til the eleventh hour?

DANNY. Because unlike you, Mr. Cobb... I'm a traditionalist. Unlike you, I refuse to stoop to coincidence. Unlike you... I still believe in plot.

> *(Once again, we hear pounding at the front door.* **NOLA** *turns and is about to open the door, when...)*

COBB. Nobody answer the door!

CHARLIE. Shouldn't we see who it is?

COBB. I know who it is!

CHARLIE. Who?

COBB. It's all of 'em.

DANNY. All of who?

COBB. The Psychotic Ukrainian Quintuplets!!

NOLA. The investors.

COBB. They're here to see the progress on the play.

(**DANNY** *stands and approaches the door.*)

DANNY. I got you into this pickle, Mr. Cobb.

(**CHARLIE** *and* **NOLA** *can't help but laugh at the word "pickle."*)

I think I should get you out of it. Dasvedanya, my friends!

(**DANNY** *walks to the door and flings it open dramatically.*)

Privet, Comrades!

(*There is no one there. There is, however, a case of vodka sitting on the threshold to the suite.* **DANNY** *picks it up and turns back into the room. The case has his name written on it.*)

COBB. What is it?

DANNY. (*Reads the card attached to the gift.*) A case of vodka – with my name on it. "Good luck with the play. – Grotzky, Grotzky, Grotzky, Grotzky and Grotzky."

(*The ceiling fan now begins to turn slowly, and gradually picks up speed until it's running properly. Everyone looks up, breathing a sigh of relief.*)

DANNY. And just like that, there's a shift in the wind.

COBB. At last, a breath of fresh air!

(*The phone rings.*)

CHARLIE. (*Into phone.*) Yello. Yep, just kicked on. (*To the room.*) It's the Super. He found a little switch no one knew about.

COBB. How convenient.

CHARLIE. (*Into phone.*) Uh-huh, uh-huh. (*To room.*) Personally he thinks we've lost our marbles. Says we've just been imagining the freak weather we've been having lately. (*He nods, quoting the caller to the assembled parties.*) "Climate change is not a *real thing*...not at the

Royal Palms Hotel." *(Into phone.)* Hold on. *(To* **NOLA***.)* Nola, he wants to know the forecast for next door?

> (**NOLA** *opens up the bedroom door, there is a flash of lightning and we hear the rumble of rain clouds.*)

NOLA. Partly sunny with scattered showers.

CHARLIE. *(Into phone.)* You hear that? Thanks. *(He's about to hang up.)* Sorry…*what?* Oh yeah, yes. Be right down. *(He hangs up.)*

COBB. What is it Charlie?

CHARLIE. Just arrived. For Mr. Jones. One Olivetti Studio 54 Portable Typewriter. There's an irate poet in the lobby who wants his back.

DANNY. I guess I should start plotting that comedy.

COBB. Sure, but don't worry so much about plot. Write a few jokes and contrive an ending. The rest'll take care of itself.

DANNY. How long do I have the room?

COBB. Take your time, kid.

DANNY. Lovely…have 'em send up some ice.

> (**NOLA** *has slinked her way over to* **CHARLIE***.*)

NOLA. Charlie, for the record. I've slept with a lot of people in this business, like…*a lot*…but I've *never* slept with an *assistant.* I'm sorry, but it's just one of my iron-clad rules.

CHARLIE. Mr. Cobb??

COBB. *(A quick beat, then…)* I guess he's due for a promotion.

> (**NOLA** *and* **CHARLIE** *canoodle, as* **COBB** *steps toward the window, where sunshine is now streaming in. He tries, and is able to jimmy the handle, throwing open the window.*)

Well, look at that? That looks to me like a bright future.

NOLA. *(Pointing.)* No, in here. Indoors. Is that…?

(Suddenly a rainbow arcs across the stage.)

A rainbow.

DANNY. Why, it's beautiful.

COBB. I sure do love the magic of theatre. And that, I think...is as good an ending as any.

(Music plays. The lights slowly fade to black.)

The End